This book has been donated by
Charlene Haines

-Author: Unexpected Heroes: The Battle for the Black Onyx
Unexpected Heroes: Birth of Victory

Keep writing!
Do not be
discouraged!
-Charlene
Haines

Unexpected Heroes

Birth of Victory

Written by Charlene Haines
Cover Illustration by Melissa Saville

authorHOUSE®

AuthorHouse™
1663 Liberty Drive
Bloomington, IN 47403
www.authorhouse.com
Phone: 1-800-839-8640

This book is a work of fiction. People, places, events, and situations are the product of the author's imagination. Any resemblance to actual persons, living or dead, or historical events, is purely coincidental.

First published by AuthorHouse 9/15/2009

ISBN: 978-1-4490-1502-2 (e)
ISBN: 978-1-4490-1501-5 (sc)

Library of Congress Control Number: 2009909212

Printed in the United States of America
Bloomington, Indiana

This book is printed on acid-free paper.

Dedicated to
Paul Bittinger, Jeff Dowdell, and Joe McGee

Heaven took you too soon

Acknowledgments

I sincerely thank the following people for their contributions and support in the creation and publication of this book:

I love and appreciate you all

My mom, Cheryl (Pooch) Haines- for the constant support and love. You are truly the greatest mother ever, and words cannot describe how grateful I am to you.

My dad, Ted Haines- for offering a helping-hand in the grammar department once again. You helped me more than you will ever realize... seriously.

My brother, Buddy Haines- for being one of the strongest people I have ever met. You are a terrific brother, and your support is always appreciated.

My Aunt, Pepper Shrout- my series continues, but began because of you.

Melissa (Reeves) Saville- for once again taking the image of the book cover from my mind and creating its exact replica. You have extreme talent, and should never let it go. Together, we will go far. Keep your chin up… we'll make it.

****Brooke (Davis) Long-*** for having a great eye in capturing a beautiful picture. You help others see the world in a better light. Keep up the great work!

****Valerie (Wright) Hurst-*** for once again anticipating the release of my book. You helped me to remember my excitement by expressing your own. You also put the word out for this book, and not only are my characters thankful for this, I am as well.

****Matthew Blevins-*** for being the greatest fan an author could ever hope for. I am happy to go through life knowing that I will always have you as a loyal reader. I will never be able to thank you enough.

****Holly and Dave Boone-*** for accepting me into your home and my written word into your son's mind. You are two of the greatest people I have ever had the pleasure of meeting. I thank you from the bottom of my heart.

****Michael Hurst-*** for your constant support in the progress of my series, and for all the honest conversations we have had. I also want to thank you for introducing me to my number one fan.

****Mike Leasure, Greg Norris, Gladys, and Joe-*** for never letting me forget the talent I possess. I want to thank you all for attending nearly every book signing event I participate in. You four are irreplaceable.

****Amber Shrout and Chris Clites-*** for being interested in the progress of my series. I know that when Drayke grows up, he will enjoy this series as much as others will.

****Frank Bittinger-*** for taking me under your wing. Together, we will fly far.

****Skip Bryner-*** for motivating me to put work before play. My readers thank you.

****Tim Jones-*** for the countless hours you have put forth in helping to create my first website.

****Heather Lloyd-*** for being the terrific person and publicist you are. Because of you, my books will be read throughout the East coast and beyond. I thank you sincerely.

***Seth Stivala-** for participating in my contest, and winning.

***The staff at Waldenbooks-** for taking a chance on an unknown writer.

***My co-workers-** for taking the time to read my books, and discussing the story with me during working hours and beyond.

***My ever-supportive myspace/facebook/high school/college friends and family-** I could not have made a few difficult decisions without you guys.

***Fozzie-** for being the greatest friend I have ever, or will ever have. You were by my side while I wrote this book. I know you'll be there next time. I love you forever.

Guide

"Unexpected Heroes: Birth of Victory" has been written in a few genres: Science Fiction; Fantasy; Action/Adventure and Mystery/Suspense. Being written for these genres, there may be words that can be quite a challenge to say. I know that the strange names in this book look very intimidating, but they're really not. It was quite fun to hear my family members trying to say these words! Although I am writing out how *I* say these words, it may be different for others. As long as you understand what I am writing, then have fun with it! I know I did! I hope that you find this guide helpful even though these words will not make sense at first. As you read; however, you may find it helpful. I sincerely hope that you enjoy this epic story and the sequels to follow. Thanks for reading!

❁ - placed throughout the book informs the reader of the change in scene/setting.

Pronunciation

XOULA - zool-la

ARTOBEALU - ar-two-be-a-lew

TRIAD- tree-ad

CEMBALOTE - sem-ba-lote

REET - reat

CALHAUSEN - cal-house-en

PIXADAIRIE - picks-a-darry

CIERO - see-air-o

LA CROIX - la-croy

KIBTELO – kib-tell-o

KEILO – key-low

RISA – ree-sa

LADAQUITTE - lad-a-quit-e

MARIETTE – mary-ett

ABOUL - a-bull

CAJHORIAN - ka-jor-y-an

The three teenagers opened their eyes and gasped in delight while they gazed around at the familiar sights of their neighborhood. Matthew sighed deeply, wiping the tear from his eye.

"Oh, we're home!" Eddie exclaimed as they started to walk up the road.

Sheila smiled at Eddie and then turned to Matthew. "You really shouldn't have left that way, you know? You should have at least given him a hug."

"Forget it," Matthew said and looked down. "That was so stupid of him anyway."

"What? Because he and Jade are having a baby?" she asked him.

"Yes!" Matthew shouted, turning to her. "And do you remember what Queen Xoula said? She said that we should never separate! And what did we do?! We separated!"

"Honestly, Matthew," Eddie started. "We're gonna go back in less than two months."

"Yeah," Matthew said and scoffed. "But he left me with the responsibility of trying to explain his disappearance to our parents!"

"It'll be fine, Matthew," Sheila assured him as they started to walk again. "We just have to think of something real quick. We have to think of something to tell them... explaining why Jeremy isn't with us."

Matthew then stopped walking suddenly and looked at Sheila. "Sheila? Can we just go back and get him? Please? I'll grab a hold of him and we can bring him back here. Please? I can't stay here without him," he pleaded, his eyes beginning to fill with tears.

Sheila sighed softly while she looked into his sorrowful face. Then, she abruptly looked around in complete confusion and panic. "Guys," she began. "Do you hear that?"

"Hear what?" Eddie asked. "All I hear is the kids playing and the birds in the tree over there."

"Yeah," she said. "That's the problem."

Eddie and Matthew looked over at her while she continued to gaze around, listening to the birds chirping and children yelling throughout the neighborhood.

"What's the big deal?" Matthew asked her.

"Well, when I left Earth the first time, you know with you guys... I stopped time," she replied. "But... somehow time has resumed here."

Eddie and Matthew immediately looked at one another. Their breathing stopped as they realized that time resuming on Earth while they were gone meant problems for them.

"Well, how long were we gone?" Matthew asked her.

"Three months!" a young girl on a bicycle suddenly said as she circled them.

"Amber!" Eddie yelled and knelt down to her. "Oh, it's so great to see you!"

"Yeah, whatever," she spoke. "But, you guys are in *big* trouble! The cops were here and everything! They thought you were dead! Where were you guys? Did you get abducted by aliens or something?"

Eddie instantly stood up and rejoined his friends. The three teenagers swallowed hard and looked at one another, struggling for an explanation. The little girl on the bicycle continued to circle them while their faces became blank. Sensing suspicion in their actions and body language, she stopped peddling her bicycle and sat on the seat to face them.

However, in that instance, the teenagers witnessed a remarkable, yet familiar incident begin to happen to the little girl. Eddie shook his head at the sight and chuckled nervously, while Sheila placed her hand over her mouth.

Matthew knelt down to the little girl and whispered, "Amber... you're glowing."

ONE

Big Trouble

"Amber, you're glowing," Matthew told her and looked up at his friends.

Sheila and Eddie continued to stare at the brilliant orange glow emitting from the little girl's body. Matthew stood up to join them by their sides, staring at her as well.

"What are you staring at?" Amber asked them, confused at their bewilderment.

"Amber, you *are* glowing," Sheila whispered to her.

"Oh, I am not," Amber scoffed and flipped her strawberry blonde braid from her shoulder.

"Yes, you are," Eddie told her and knelt down to her. "Look," he said and pointed to her hand resting upon the handlebars.

Amber's eyes widened when she witnessed what the teenagers had noticed. The radiant aura surrounded her as it had Sheila on Artobealu.

"Wh- what is it?" Amber asked them, her voice shaking with fear.

"You're a Triad," Sheila revealed quietly.

"What is that?" Amber asked her, looking up into her face.

"It's nothing to be afraid of," Eddie assured her, standing to his feet. "Trust us."

"All I can say is," Matthew began and placed his hand to his forehead. "It must be something in the water here. I mean, we've got... apparently *two* Traids in the same neighborhood... along with an evil Cembalote. Am I missing anything?"

"It *is* quite odd," Eddie agreed.

Just then, the glow surrounding Amber disappeared. Eddie, Sheila, and Matthew looked at her while she remained sitting on the bicycle.

"Why are you staring at me like that? Jeez," Amber asked and placed her feet on the pedals of her bicycle.

"You're not glowing anymore," Eddie answered.

"Good," she said. "Then I can go home."

"Wait! Amber... you can't go yet!" Eddie said and stood in front of her bicycle, prohibiting her from moving forward.

"You can't tell me what to do," she replied, looking up at him.

"Amber," Sheila whispered and knelt down to her side. "Something is happening to you. I don't know why or how... but it is."

Amber sighed and shook her head. "You three are nuts," she claimed and pushed her bicyle through Eddie. "I don't know what you're talking about."

The three teenagers watched as she peddled away from them, shaking her head in denial.

"Okay," Eddie said and took a deep breath. "We all saw that, right?"

"Uh-huh," Matthew agreed.

"Absolutely," Sheila agreed as well.

"Then... how do we explain that?" he asked them.

"I told you," Matthew answered. "There's something not right with this neighborhood."

"Matthew's right," Sheila stated. "It is strange that a lot seems to be happening in the same place."

"Well, I know one thing," Eddie said and looked around at the houses in the neighborhood. "We're all in big trouble."

Matthew and Sheila's breathing ceased. They had remembered about time resuming while they were absent.

"We need to think of a story... and quickly," Sheila suggested and turned to her friends. "We need to account for Jeremy and Shane."

"Well, I've decided that I am going to tell the truth about Shane," Eddie revealed to them.

"What? You can't do that!" Matthew disputed.

"Why not?" Eddie asked him. "I can't let Olivia Aramay go on without knowing."

"What are you going to tell her? You can't tell her about where we've been! They'll think we're nuts!" Matthew argued.

"Don't worry, Matthew," Eddie assured him. "I'm not going to say anything about what just happened to us. I'll make something up."

"Well, whatever we do... we've got to do it now, so that we all have the same story," Sheila told them.

"Okay," Eddie began and took a deep breath.

At that very moment, the teenagers heard a loud shriek. They immediately looked up to discover what had happened. There, standing a few feet away, was the twins' mother.

"Matthew! Where have you been?!" she yelled and ran toward him. She embraced him tightly while his friends looked on.

"Mom!" Matthew called out, hugging her with all of his might.

Eddie and Sheila stood back and looked at one another timidly. Their hearts raced and their breathing increased while they stuggled for a believeable explanation for their disappearance.

"Where is Jeremy?" Matthew's mother asked, releasing her grip from him.

"Uh.. um," Matthew began and looked at his friends.

"Where is he, Matthew?" his mother asked once again.

"He's... he's not here," Matthew answered quietly.

His mother paused. She then whispered to him, "where were you?"

"I'm sorry, Mom," he answered quietly. "But, I can't tell you where we were."

Matthew's mother scoffed and turned toward Eddie and Sheila. "Perhaps you two can tell me?" she asked them.

Eddie and Sheila lowered their heads. "We're sorry," Eddie answered.

"You're sorry?" she asked, her voice growing louder. "Someone is going to give me answers... and I mean, right now!"

The teenagers looked at one another. Sheila then sighed and spoke, "you wouldn't understand."

"Try me," she demanded.

"Mom," Matthew interrupted. "Jeremy is not coming home... I can't tell you where he is, or where we've been. But, you have to trust that he is okay."

She shook her head and grabbed Matthew's hand. "Matthew, I am happy that you are home and safe... but I need to know where your brother is."

"He really is okay, Mrs. Germaine," Eddie whsipered and placed his hand on her shoulder.

"Eddie," she began and turned toward him. "You and Sheila should go home. Your families are worried sick."

"Yes, ma'am," Eddie replied and looked at Matthew.

Matthew slowly nodded his head and sighed. Eddie smiled at his friend and turned to walk in the direction of his house. Sheila remained standing on the road.

"Go on home, Sheila," Matthew's mother instructed.

Sheila sighed and turned away to walk toward her house. As she turned to walk away, she stopped suddenly. Slowly, she turned around and watched as Matthew and his mother approached the steps to his house. Eddie turned around as well and swallowed hard. He raised his hand up to wave at Sheila, who slowly returned the gesture.

He watched as she turned around once again and walked in the direction of her house. His hand began to shake with fear as he began to realize his own fate was uncertain.

Walking past Shane's house enroute to his own, Eddie shuddered uncontrollably. Stopping in the middle of the road, he turned to face the home of his former friend. He inhaled deeply and stepped toward the sidewalk leading to the front door. The pounding of his heart increased with each step he took. Slowly, he grew closer to the porch, pondering how Olivia Aramay would accept the news of her only son's untimely death.

When he finally reached the front door, he nervously knocked twice. Patiently, he waited for the door to open, revealing a distraught mother's face.

"Eddie?" Olivia Aramay whispered as she opened the door for him. "My God!"

She embraced him tightly, while he struggled to find the courage to return the favor. His arms wrapped around her as his mind filled with images of Shane, and the horrible death he experienced.

"Come in, please," Olivia invited, opening the door wider for him. "Where is Shane?" she finally asked, looking out into the yard, hoping to find him approaching as well.

"That's what I came to tell you," he answered, his voice trembling.

"Tell me what?" she asked, closing the door behind her.

"Mrs. Aramay," he began. "Please sit down."

"Eddie," she said quietly. "Why do you want me to sit down?"

"Please," he begged.

Olivia hesitated at first, but then obliged the young man's request. "Okay."

Eddie sat down next to her and turned to face her. "There was an accident," he began.

"Accident?" she whispered. "What accident? Where were you kids?"

"Please," he spoke softly. "There was an accident... and Shane was killed."

Olivia's facial expression immediately changed to sorrow when she heard of her son's misfortune.

"Killed?" she asked, looking away from him.

"Yes," he answered.

"How?" she asked, placing her hand to her mouth.

"He fell," Eddie replied.

Olivia became silent. Her eyes collected tears while her mind filled with memories of her son. Eddie reached for her hand to comfort her, but she pulled it away quickly.

"Where is he, Eddie?" she asked, her voice growing deep with anger.

Eddie sighed deeply and replied, "gone."

"Gone where?" she asked, turning to face him.

"He's far away, Mrs. Aramay," he answered. "Far away."

"Eddie," Olivia began and looked into his eyes. "I want you to tell me where my son is."

"I can't," he whispered and looked down.

"You will," she said sternly and placed her hand on his chin. With a quick movement, she pulled his chin toward her. "You will tell *me*, or you will tell the police. The choice is yours."

Eddie's jaw dropped slightly when she said this. He swallowed hard and took a deep breath.

"I can't," he replied quietly as a tear formed in his eye. "I'm so sorry."

Olivia chuckled quietly and released her hand from his chin. She stood up and walked to the door. Opening it, she said, "you go on home now. The police will be by in a little while."

Eddie stood to his feet and walked to the door. "I'm sorry," he whispered.

"Uh-huh," she said and wiped the tear from her eye.

Eddie looked down to the floor and walked through the door. Quickly, he walked in the direction of his home. As he walked down the driveway, he heard a faint siren in the distance. His breathing increased as the siren grew closer.

He opened the door to his house and looked around in the kitchen. Just then, his father opened the door from the basement and faced his son. The two stood in complete silence, staring at one another.

His father's eyes began to form tears as he approached him. He wrapped his arms around his son and sobbed loudly. Eddie immediately hugged his father tightly, closing his eyes as tears streamed down his face.

"Joe? What is it?" Eddie's mother's voice was heard from the livingroom.

She walked through the entrance to the kitchen and gasped when she watched her husband hugging their missing son.

"Eddie!" she yelled and ran to them.

She immediately grabbed Eddie and held onto him tightly, sobbing as well. They continued to embrace one another, weeping in relief.

"Where were you?" his mother asked, looking up into Eddie's face.

"Oh, Mom," Eddie replied and sobbed, holding her tightly.

"Eddie? What is it? Where were you?" she asked, stroking the back of his head gently.

Eddie merely sobbed into his mother's chest. His father rubbed her back while she held onto Eddie. Suddenly, a knock was suddenly heard on the front door. Eddie immediately looked up in the direction of the door. His parents noticed that his breathing had ceased completely.

"What is it?" his mother asked him.

"Mom," he whispered and turned his head to look at her. "I didn't mean to kill Shane."

His parents instantly paused. His father looked down at the floor and sighed deeply.

"What did you do, Edward?" he asked him.

"It was an accident," Eddie answered quietly.

"You killed Shane?" his mother asked him. "You killed your best friend?"

Eddie shook his head and replied, "he wasn't my best friend."

The knock was heard once again on the front door. That time; however, followed by a voice demanding, "open up! This is the police!"

Eddie's father walked over to the door and looked out. "It *is* the police," he informed his family.

"Dad, please," Eddie begged. "Mrs. Aramay called them. She thinks I'm hiding something."

"I am getting that impression as well, Edward," his father replied and opened the door.

Three police officers walked through the door and approached Eddie. The first officer handed Eddie's father a piece of paper.

"I am going to take your son in for questioning," he explained.

"Regarding what?" his father asked.

"The disappearance of Shane Aramay," the police officer answered and grabbed Eddie's arm, pulling him away from his mother.

"Wait!" Eddie's mother called out. "But, he just got here!"

"I need you both to come down to the station to be present during questioning," the police officer ordered, fastening handcuffs around Eddie's wrists.

Eddie's father nodded his head and watched the police officer lead Eddie to a patrol car parked in the driveway. The officer assisted Eddie into the back seat and shut the door. Eddie's tear-filled eyes looked out the window at his parents watching from the doorway.

Arriving at the police station, the same police officer that had taken Eddie from his house led him through the door and into an interrogation room. He sat him down in a chair and removed the handcuffs.

"Sorry about that," he said, placing the handcuffs on the table in front of Eddie. "Procedure."

Eddie was silent. He nodded his head slightly and stared at the table before him. The police officer sighed and sat down in the chair across from him.

"It seems to me like you've been through quite a lot," he began. "So, I can understand if you want to get through this quickly."

Eddie remained silent.

"Look, son," the police officer said and leaned closer. "Two of your friends are missing. And, we are not getting any information out of the other two kids that suddenly appeared with you after three months. Kidnapping and murder are serious offenses. You understand that, don't you, son?"

Eddie sighed deeply and continued to sit in silence.

"Okay," the officer whispered. "I thought I would give you the chance to clear things up right away. But, we will just wait for your parents then."

A few minutes later, the door to the interrogation room opened. Eddie's parents walked through and sat down next to their son.

"Thank you for coming," the police officer said to them, standing to his feet. "I am Detective Bud Linus," he said and shook their hands.

"Joe Miles," Eddie's father said and shook the detective's hand. "This is my wife, Angela."

"Hello," she whispered and shook his hand as well.

"Okay," the detective said and sat down. "It has come to my attention that your son and four neighborhood teens went missing three months ago, correct?"

"That is correct," Joe answered. "We reported them missing... along with the Germaines, the Greises... and Olivia Aramay."

"Right. But now, they have re-appeared... minus two," the detective said and opened his notebook. "A Jeremy Germaine, and a Shane Aramay. These are friends of your son's?"

"Yes," Eddie's mother answered.

"Okay, now we're getting somewhere," the detective began and cleared his throat. "Eddie," he addressed him. "Where did you and your friends go for three months?"

Eddie was silent.

"Edward, answer the man's question," Eddie's father demanded.

He remained silent, staring at the tabletop.

"Mr. Miles, I believe that your son may be suffering from what is called post-traumatic stress disorder. Wherever he went, and whatever he did... must've been terrifying," Detective Linus informed him.

"Terrifying?" Eddie's mother asked, looking at her son's blank stare. "Where could he have gone?"

"Not sure," the detective replied.

"Joe," Eddie's mother began, looking at her husband. "Could they have been kidnapped by terrorists and taken to Iraq?"

Eddie's father scoffed and shook his head. "I don't think so, Angela."

"Well," the detective interrupted. "That is not so uncommon. Things like that happen a lot. Children are particular favorites of certain criminals... I'll just leave it at that."

Instantly, Eddie's parents became silent. They lowered their heads and each took their son's hand. Detective Linus cleared his throat and motioned to the police officer standing outside the door.

"Yes, Detective?" the officer asked when he opened the door.

"Coffee," Detective Linus whispered.

"Yes, sir," the officer said and closed the door behind him.

"Eddie," the detective began and looked into his face. "In order to help you and your friends, you must tell me what happened."

He remained silent.

"Alright, the next step now is to have a pychiatrist evaluate your son," the detective addressed Eddie's parents.

"A shrink?" Eddie's dad asked. "Do you really think that is necessary?"

"Absolutely," he answered. "Your son is not going to talk to me about what happened, and in order to locate the other two, I must have answers. If they are in any kind of trouble... Well, imagine how you would feel if every one of the missing teenagers returned... except for your son."

"You'll never find them," Eddie abruptly whispered.

"What's that?" the detective asked.

"You will never find them," Eddie repeated, looking into the detective's face.

"Oh? And why is that?"

"Because- because they're far, far away," Eddie answered.

"Far away as in... California?" the detective asked.

"Far away as in... not on Earth," Eddie replied and smirked at the detective.

Detective Linus sat back in his chair and looked away from Eddie. He shook hs head and sighed.

"I will have a therapist brought in first thing in the morning," the detective said and motioned to a different officer standing at the door.

"But," Eddie's mother spoke. "Can he come home?"

"No," the detective answered and whispered into the police officer's ear. "Okay?" he asked him.

"Right away," the officer replied and walked through the door.

"So, he has to stay here?" she asked him.

"Yes," he said and stood up. "We really don't know anything about the past three months in this young man's life. Therefore, he must stay here until we have answers."

"Now, wait a minute," Eddie's father said and stood up as well. "You have nothing to hold him on. He wasn't charged with anything!"

"How about kidnapping and murder? You wanna start with that?" the detective said and reached for the doorknob.

"I didn't kill anyone!" Eddie screamed and looked up at the detective.

"That's not what Olivia Aramay is saying," the detective said and scoffed. "She said that you confessed to her."

"I didn't confess! It was an accident!" Eddie yelled.

"Uh-huh," the detective said and released his grip on the doorknob. "Are you ready to talk now?"

"No," Eddie answered. "I can't tell anyone anything! You know why? Because no one will believe us!"

"Us?" the detective asked. "So, your friends are involved as well, huh?"

Eddie became silent once again.

"I see," Detective Linus said and turned the doorknob. "I will see you in the morning, then."

He motioned for two police officers to place the handcuffs on Eddie. His parents stood by and watched helplessly as the officers led him out of the interrogation room and down the hallway to his jail cell.

"Matthew, please tell me what is going on," his mother begged, sitting next to him in another adjacent interrogation room.

"Mom, I can't," he answered. "Please."

"At least tell me where you went, please," she whispered.

"That's what I can't tell you," he replied. "You wouldn't understand."

"I may if you'd let me," she said.

"Trust me, you wouldn't."

The door to the interrogation room suddenly opened and Detective Linus walked through. He took a sip of his coffee and sat down in the chair across from Matthew and his mother.

"I'm Detective Bud Linus," he said and reached for Matthew's mother's hand.

"Valerie Germaine," she said and shook his hand.

"Is there a Mr. Germaine?" he asked her, flipping the pages of his notebook.

"He's out of town for business," she answered and looked down. "I've called him."

Matthew looked over at his mother and took her hand. Detective Linus continued to flip through the pages of his notebook while Matthew and his mother watched nervously.

"Your friend Eddie Miles will not disclose what happened," the detective finally spoke. He looked up at Matthew and sighed. "So, should we expect the same treatment from you?"

"Yes," Matthew replied.

"Your brother is missing," the detective said. "As well as Shane Aramay."

"My brother is fine," Matthew said and chuckled. "As for Shane..."

"As for Shane what?"

"He's better off."

Detective Linus chuckled slightly and wrote down Matthew's statement in his notebook.

"Are you admitting that Shane was killed?" he asked him, taking another sip from his coffee cup.

"Yes," Matthew answered.

"And... who would be responsible?"

"No one," Matthew said and held onto his mother's hand tightly. "It was an accident."

"You know," the detective began and leaned closer to him. "You're quite a bit different than your friend Eddie; he sat there nearly the whole time and did not speak."

"So?"

"All I am saying is... I do not believe that he could have been responsible for Shane's death."

Matthew became silent.

"Your statement, so far, portrays you as one who is arrogant, immature, and quite possibly the one responsible for Shane's murder."

"Now, what a minute," his mother spoke up. "These kids had nothing to do with whatever happened to Shane."

"How do you know? Were you there?" the detective asked her.

She became silent as well.

"That's what I thought," he said and cleared his throat. "Now, Olivia Aramay needs answers, and quite frankly I do not blame her. You kids disappear for three months... and return without your brother and without Shane. But, the thing that astounds me the most is... no one seems to want to offer an explanation. There are two teenagers missing; one possibly dead, and the other... well, no one really said much about Jeremy. So, how about it? Do you want to tell me about your brother?"

"No, I don't," Matthew answered. "Whatever we tell you, you will not believe. You've already got it in your head that Shane was murdered, which is not true! God only knows what you're thinking about Jeremy."

"I have to think about everything logically, Matthew. And logically speaking, Eddie admitted to Olivia Aramay that Shane was killed. You, yourself just admitted that he is dead. So, we have to rationalize about Jeremy's whereabouts."

"I'm telling you, Jeremy is fine! I would never hurt my brother!"

"Understand," he said. "I'm sure that's what you said about Shane at one point."

Detective Linus then stood up and approached the door. He sighed and shook his head.

"We're detaining Eddie overnight for a psychiatric evaluation in the morning. You are free to go... just stay close," he said and walked through the door.

Sheila sat in a separate interrogation room with her parents. They sat in silence, staring at the table in front of them. Detective Linus then opened the door and entered, sitting in the chair across from them.

"I am Detective Bud Linus," he said and reached his hand out. "Thank you for your patience."

"Dr. Steven Greise," Sheila's father said and shook the detective's hand.

"Veronica," Sheila's mother said and shook the detective's hand as well.

"Good," the detective said and flipped through his notebook. "How are you doing, Sheila?" he asked her.

"How do you think?" she asked, rolling her eyes.

"Straighten up," her father said quietly, in a strict voice.

"I just spoke to your friend, Matthew," Detective Linus began. "He authenticated Eddie's claim that Shane Aramay is dead. Would you like to tell me how? Why? Where you kids disappeared to for three months?"

"No," Sheila answered.

Sheila's father then cleared his throat loudly. Sheila immediately shifted in her chair and looked across the table at the detective.

"No, I don't," she said and smiled slightly at the detective.

"I don't know why you kids are trying so hard to be difficult," the detective said and wrote in his notebook. "All you have to do is tell the truth. Ever hear the saying 'the truth shall set you free'?" he asked and looked up at her.

"I have," she replied.

"So, tell the truth, Sheila. Set yourself free."

"I am free," she said. "And so are my friends. We did no wrong; Shane very much deserved what he got."

Sheila's parents groaned when those words left her lips. Detective Linus chuckled and wrote her statement down in his notebook.

"It was intentional, then?" he asked her.

"No," she answered. "It was self-defense."

"You're going to go with that, then? Self-defense?" he asked.

"That's the truth, Detective. Shane was trying to kill us."

"Your friend was trying to kill you? In a place that you won't disclose, right? What did Eddie say? Oh, yeah... far, far away," he chuckled.

"Yeah," she answered. "Far away."

"Not on Earth, right? Mars perhaps? Maybe Jupiter?"

Sheila groaned and rolled her eyes.

"Detective," Sheila's father interrupted. "Can we move along with this? I have a meeting to get to in an hour."

"Sure, Dr. Greise," the detective said and chuckled. "Sheila, this is what's going to happen," he addressed her. "Your friend Matthew has been released to his mother, but Eddie is staying here overnight."

"Overnight? Why?" she asked him.

"Psychiatric evaluation," he answered. "I believe that he has post traumatic stress."

"Oh, he does not," she argued. "He just knows that if he tells the whole truth, he'll be deemed insane! The same with us! If Matthew or I tell you what happened, where we were... you'd have us locked away!"

"Doesn't have to be like that, Sheila," he said quietly. "But, you'd have to trust me."

"Trust you? You're already thinking Eddie's crazy because he said Shane isn't on Earth!" she said.

Detective Linus was silent.

"Now, that's what *I* thought," she said and stood up.

Sheila and her parents walked through the door of the interrogation room and toward the exit. Suddenly, Sheila stopped.

"I'll be right back," she said to them and started walking down the hall.

"Where are you going?" her mother asked.

Sheila did not answer. She continued to walk down the hall until she reached a large door that appeared to be locked. She took a deep breath and closed her eyes. Instantaneously, time stopped.

"Oh, yes," she whispered and smiled.

She searched around the vicinity for the guard responsible for holding the keys to the door. When she located him, she grabbed the dangling keys from his pocket and walked back to the door. Quickly, she unlocked the door and entered.

She then walked down the hallway separating the jail cells and searched for her friend. Finally, she found him in the very last cell.

His face was sullen and morose. He was frozen in time, but Sheila could still see the emotion behind his eyes. She unlocked the door and walked through, sitting down at his side.

She then closed her eyes. As time resumed, she grabbed his arm. He was instantly startled and looked into her face. She smiled and closed her eyes once again.

"Sheila?" he asked and hugged her tightly.

"It's me," she whispered and held him.

"Time has stopped?"

"Yes," she answered.

He released his embrace from her and leaned up to look into her face. He sighed deeply and asked, "where's Matthew?"

"They sent him home," she answered and smiled at him.

"They want to give me a psych exam," he informed her.

"I know," she said and stood to her feet. "That joke of a detective thinks we're murderers."

"No," Eddie said and stood to his feet as well. "He thinks *I'm* a murderer."

"Eddie," she said and placed her hands on his upper arms. "I respect you for what you tried to do for Olivia Aramay. But, you really shouldn't have."

Eddie chuckled and said, "yeah… I should have."

"I guess you did what you felt was right," Sheila said and chuckled as well.

Eddie sighed deeply and looked out into the hallway. The criminals in the jail cells were completely still, as well as the guards.

"What are we going to do now?" he asked her.

"Let's get Matthew," she replied.

"Then, what?" he whispered, looking back at her.

Sheila was silent.

"Sheila," he began and walked toward her. "If you break me out, I'll be a fugitive. Not only will I have escaped… but that pretty much proves guilt."

"Eddie, they're talking *murder*," she explained. "And it's not just Shane. They think something happened to Jeremy, too."

"Wow," he said and looked down at the floor of the jail cell. "That's double murder."

"Yeah," she whispered.

"Maybe I should have told the truth… instead of being silent," he said quietly.

"No… it would be the same thing, Eddie. They won't believe us, no matter what we say."

"We need to make an educated decision," Eddie told her and looked out into the hallway again. "We need to talk to Matthew."

"You're right. Where would he be now?"

"Home," he replied and smiled at her.

Eddie and Sheila arrived outside of Matthew's house and stepped out of Sheila's parents' car.

"When did you learn to drive?" Sheila asked Eddie as she closed the passenger side door.

"My dad taught me... wow that seems like forever ago" he answered and closed his door as well.

They walked up the steps that led to Matthew's house and stood on the porch. Sheila took a deep breath and opened the front door. Slowly, they walked through and searched the living room for any sign of Matthew or his mother.

"Sheila," Eddie called out from the kitchen. "I found him."

Sheila walked into the kitchen and looked at Matthew, sitting across from his mother at the kitchen table.

"Look at her," she whispered to Eddie, regarding Matthew's mother.

Her face was damp with tears, and her facial expression spoke of the sorrow she was experiencing at the very moment Sheila had stopped time.

"She misses Jeremy," Eddie whispered, and knelt down to the twins' mother. "And we won't tell her anything."

"We can't," Sheila whispered and knelt down to her as well. "You know what would happen if we told the truth."

"I know," he said and sighed. "I wouldn't believe our story, either."

"Well, I am going to grab Matthew... hold on to me," she said and gently touched Matthew's arm.

She closed her eyes and resumed time. Without hesitation, she stopped time once again. Matthew exhaled deeply and wiped the tears from his eyes. He looked up at his mother and gasped. His eyes then caught the sight of Sheila and Eddie.

"Oh!" he exclaimed and hugged Sheila tightly. "We are so dead!"

"No," Eddie said and stood to his feet. "But, we need to make a decision regarding what to do here."

"What do you mean?" Matthew asked him, letting go of Sheila.

"Detective Linus has it in for me," Eddie explained. "He thinks I am responsible for Shane's murder... and now, they think Jeremy is a victim also."

"Well, what can we do? I mean, we've got to deal with this, right?" Matthew asked, wiping his damp cheek.

"Matthew, what Eddie is getting at... is that we need to decided whether or not to go back... to Artobealu," Sheila said.

"No way," Matthew protested. "Do you guys even know that Jeremy and I missed our birthday? We're sixteen now, and I didn't even know it!"

"I'm sorry, Matthew," Eddie spoke.

"And, what are we going to do about school? It's now September 24th… and we've missed almost a whole month. We're never going to get caught up," he said.

"Matthew, I don't think you're thinking about the bigger picture here," Sheila said and sighed. "Eddie is going to be tried for murder."

"No, he won't," Matthew argued. "They can't prove it! There is no body! They can't prove murder without a body… its textbook criminology."

"It doesn't work like that," Eddie said and looked out the window. "I've pretty much confessed to Shane's mom… so, they'll get me for that."

"We told you not to tell," Matthew said and stood up.

"They would have asked eventually," Eddie said and turned around to face him. "They would have thought it was strange that we came back… without Jeremy and Shane."

"Eddie," Matthew began. "Look at my mother's face," he said and pointed to her, frozen in time. "It is killing her that I won't tell her about Jeremy. I can't tell her about our powers… I can't tell her that she's going to be a grandmother… I can't tell her about Shane. And, I certainly can't leave her again."

"I understand, Matthew," Eddie whispered. "But if we leave… you'll be the one to take the fall."

Matthew was silent.

"He's right," Sheila spoke. "If we disappear again, Detective Linus will be all over you. We wanted to talk to you about going back… because we didn't want to leave you here."

Matthew sighed and looked into his mother's face. He walked over to her and wiped away the tears on her cheek. Gently, he kissed her forehead and whispered, "I love you, Mom."

TWO

Return

Eddie, Sheila, and Matthew stood outside in a circle and held hands. Matthew's hands shook with anticipation as he thought of seeing his brother once again. At that moment; however, a thought crossed Eddie's mind.

"Sheila, wait," he spoke up and released his grip from her hand.

"What is it?" she asked, releasing her grip from Matthew's hand.

"What about Amber Drayke?" he asked of the little neighborhood girl.

"We can't take her," Matthew said, facing him. "Are you nuts? Do you want to add kidnapping of a child to the list of charges against you?"

"It won't be kidnapping," Eddie assured him. "Sheila, you can stop time here again, right?"

"Yes," she said quietly. "If it'll work this time."

"Okay, then," Eddie said and walked down the steps toward the road.

"Where are you going?" Matthew called out.

"To get Amber Drayke," he replied. "There's something going on with that girl... and I feel like we should find out."

Matthew looked over at Sheila. She shrugged her shoulders and followed Eddie. Matthew scoffed and shook his head.

When they reached Amber's house, they stood outside for a moment in silence. The world was completely silent, which caused a feeling of uneasiness to rush over the teenagers while they contemplated their next move.

"I want to tell you guys," Eddie began, quietly. "If time doesn't stay frozen after we've gone… I'll take complete blame for what we're about to do."

Matthew and Sheila remained silent. They merely nodded their heads, agreeing with Eddie's statement.

The three teenagers then walked to the front door of Amber's house. Eddie reached for the doorknob and turned it slowly. The latch clicked and the door opened.

"Matthew, check the back… Sheila, check the living room. I'll check the kitchen," Eddie instructed.

They each dispersed to their designated area and began to search for the little girl. Eddie walked passed her parents cooking dinner. He chuckled and entered the hallway leading to the bedrooms. He opened each door slowly, looking for her. Finally, he located her in her parent's bedroom.

"Guys!" he called out to his friends. "I've found her!"

Matthew and Sheila reached him and looked into the bedroom at the girl, lying on her stomach watching the television.

"Okay, Sheila," Eddie said and walked over to Amber. "Whenever you're ready."

"Eddie, are you sure about this?" Sheila asked.

"Yes," he replied. "For all we know… she may be another one of your sisters."

"Okay," She whispered and touched Amber on her shoulder.

As quickly as before, she resumed time. She stopped time again, just as quick. Amber blinked her eyes and scoffed when she noticed her television program was paused, frozen in time by Sheila. She remained unaware of her visitors while she pressed the buttons on the remote control, struggling to turn the channel.

"Amber," Sheila spoke softly.

Immediately, the little girl looked up at them and screamed at the top of her lungs. The teenagers instantly held their ears in pain while she continued to scream.

"Amber, stop!" Matthew yelled out.

Amber opened her eyes and looked at the three teenagers standing before her. Her breathing had increased in panic, but seemed to slow down at that point.

"What are you doing here?" Amber asked them, standing up from the bed.

"We need you to come with us," Sheila answered. "We can't explain a whole lot right now, but you really need to trust us."

"Uh, no," Amber replied and pushed past the teenagers.

She walked into the hallway and approached the kitchen. Eddie, Sheila, and Matthew continued to stand in the bedroom. A moment later, Amber entered the room again.

"What is wrong with my parents?" she asked them.

"They're frozen in time," Matthew answered.

"Oh," she said and walked over to the bed again.

The teenagers watched as she turned her attention back to the paused television. She grunted in frustration while pressing down hard on the remote control, desperate to change the channel. Eddie looked at Matthew and Sheila and shrugged his shoulders.

"Amber, don't you want to ask us anything?" he asked, walking toward her.

"No," she replied. "This is just a dream. I am dreaming… so, I may as well try to watch something interesting."

"Okay," Eddie said and turned to his friends. "Sheila?"

She nodded her head as she and Matthew approached Eddie and Amber. Eddie reached for Amber's hand and held it gently.

"What are you doing?" she asked him.

"It's just a dream," he answered and smiled at her.

When they had made complete contact with one another, Sheila closed her eyes. Amber gasped frightfully as the sight of gray and white lights flashed in front of her.

"Don't be afraid, Amber," Matthew assured her. "This is normal."

"Okay," she said, holding onto his hand tightly.

She groaned in pain as they traveled through space and time, causing the air to reach freezing temperatures, and creating a deafening howl of blowing wind around them. Matthew felt her small trembling hand clinch his tighter and tighter at the increasing discomfort.

As the gray and white flashes amplified suddenly, Amber gasped and clamped her eyes shut. The air surrounding her began to warm drastically as the terrifying screams of the time warp subdued. At this point, Amber felt comfortable enough to finally open her eyes. Instantly, she gasped at the sight of a beautiful new world before her. She released Matthew's hand and took a few steps forward.

Eddie, Sheila, and Matthew gazed around as well. Artobealu remained as beautiful as when they departed. The teenagers watched Amber continue to explore the unique world she had been brought to.

"Where are we?" she asked them.

"This is Artobealu," Matthew answered, approaching her.

"It's wonderful," she said and turned toward the teenagers. "Why did you bring me here?"

Eddie sighed and knelt down to face her. "We want you to meet someone very special to us. We think she will be able to explain what is happening to you."

"Nothing's happening to me," Amber scoffed.

"Something did happen," Eddie told her. "You saw it too."

Amber sighed and nodded her head. Matthew reached down and took her hand.

"Come on," he whispered.

Amber held his hand and followed the teenagers to a giant structure that stood at the end of the road. Nervously, she looked around at the large trees and plant life. Strange screeching noises were heard emerging from the forest to her left. Immediately, the teenagers stopped walking and turned their heads in the direction of the sounds.

"What is that?" Eddie asked, pulling Amber behind him.

"Not sure I've heard that before," Matthew answered and stood in front of Amber as well.

"Well, we should probably keep going to the castle," Sheila suggested. "Maybe Jeremy or Jade can tell us what those strange noises are."

"Uh, how would they know, Sheila?" Matthew asked her, turning to face her. "We haven't even been gone a day."

"He's right," Eddie said. "We just left from here like... six hours ago."

"Okay," Sheila spoke and took Amber's hand. "We're going."

Matthew and Eddie followed the girls to the castle. As they stood in front of the marvelous structure, Eddie knocked on the door loudly. A moment later, the door opened, revealing an odd-looking creature. The creature was dressed in black, with a gold sash draped over his shoulder. His eyes were large and inviting, and his hair stood on end with green beads woven through the tendrils.

"Humans," the creature spoke in a wheezy voice.

"Yes," Eddie replied. "We're humans."

"What do you want?" the creature asked.

In that instance, Matthew pushed Eddie aside and stood in front of the creature. Immediately, the creature gasped and bowed down at Matthew's feet.

"Forgive me, King," the creature begged.

Matthew scoffed and turned to his friends. "King?"

"I guess he thinks you're Jeremy," Eddie whispered.

"Oh," Matthew said and chuckled. "On your feet," he ordered to the creature.

"King," the creature answered and stood to his feet instantly.

Matthew chuckled and turned to his friends. "Here we go," he said to them.

The creature backed away from the door, allowing Eddie, Sheila, and Amber to enter. Matthew walked in front of his friends and gasped at the amazing sights within the castle. His friends walking behind him did the same.

"Jeez, I don't remember seeing any of this," Eddie said, while he continued to gaze at the wonderful exhibits.

The friends had walked into the heart of the castle: a large room in the shape of an octagon. The roof stood hundreds of feet above, with balconies of each floor overlooking a giant silver fountain sitting in the center of the ground floor.

Eddie walked over to the fountain and looked down at the pool of silver liquid. He smiled and looked up at the hundreds of floors above them. At the highest point, a skylight provided daylight to the plant life within the room.

"Amazing, isn't it?" a very familiar voice asked.

Eddie and the others instantly looked up to see Jeremy standing in the doorway of a room on the ground floor. To their utter dismay, he was dressed in completely different clothing then when they had last seen him. He wore black boots, with loose-fitting caramel colored pants. A black belt wrapped around his waist with a large silver belt buckle and a shiny sword attached at the side. A maroon vest with gold lining covered his dark green tunic. Atop his short dark hair, he wore a beautiful gold crown with multi-colored gems scattered throughout.

His brother and friends continued to stare at him in complete silence. He chuckled and walked toward them, scuffing his feet upon the marble floor.

"Where have you guys been?" he finally asked them, running his finger along the edge of the fountain.

"Uh," Matthew began and walked over to him. "Why are you dressed like that?"

"Because I am king," Jeremy answered. "Jade and I were married."

Matthew instantly laughed and looked at the others. "They were married," he said to them and turned to his brother once again. "You were married?"

"Yeah," he answered. "We waited for three months… we figured you guys would be back before you started school."

The others immediately fell silent.

"Guys? I'm sorry… but we waited for you," Jeremy said quietly.

"Wait!" Matthew shouted and sat on the edge of the silver fountain. "What do you mean you waited three months?!"

"We waited for you guys," Jeremy answered.

"We just left here, Jeremy," Eddie spoke up. "Like… six hours ago."

"You were here? Why didn't you find me?" Jeremy asked, excitedly.

"No… we just left after… after Shane was killed," Matthew explained. "You know, after you and I argued."

"Oh," Jeremy said and laughed. "That was six months ago," he said, laughing.

"No, Jeremy," Sheila interrupted. "That was today."

Jeremy continued to laugh at the others, assuming that their claim was a joke. Matthew stood up and walked over, placing his hand on his brother's shoulder.

"Jeremy," he began. "I am so sorry about that fight... but we're telling the truth. You see? We're still wearing the same clothes."

Jeremy's laughs ceased as he opened his eyes and looked at his friends. They stood before him, thinking that *his* claim was a joke.

"You guys aren't kidding," he said and cleared his throat. "Huh."

"No, we're not," Matthew replied. "We're in big trouble back home... so, Eddie and Sheila thought that it would be best to come back here."

"Big trouble?" Jeremy asked quietly, sitting on the edge of the fountain.

"Yeah," Matthew answered. "Eddie's going to go to jail for killing Shane. And our parents went nuts because we were gone for three months."

Jeremy was silent.

"Oh, and they think you're a victim as well," Matthew added. "Eddie's going down for Shane's murder and your disappearance."

"But," Jeremy began and sighed. "Didn't you tell them where I was?"

"No! We couldn't tell them anything about... anything!" Matthew shouted. "They'd think we're insane if we told them everything!"

"But... I thought Sheila stopped time," Jeremy whispered, lowering his head.

"I did," Sheila replied. "But it didn't work."

"So, where have you been for six months?" Jeremy asked them, looking up.

"We told you," Matthew answered. "It's only been six hours since we left here."

"That's impossible," Jeremy argued, standing to his feet. "It's been six months!"

"No, it hasn't," Matthew said, walking over to Eddie. "When we returned to Earth, Eddie told Olivia Aramay about Shane, we were questioned by the police, and now we're here again."

"You don't believe me," Jeremy said and walked over to a door across from them. "Maybe you'll believe this."

The others stood and watched as Jeremy opened the door. He entered the room and emerged a few seconds later with Jade on his arm. Eddie, Sheila, and Matthew looked at her in disbelief. The beautiful Triad-turned-human approached them slowly, with Jeremy at her side.

Her shimmering green gown flowed upon the floor as she walked. Her long red hair was pulled back in a long braid, as a glistening crown rested on the top of her head. Her midsection; however, was quite larger than it had been the last time the teenagers saw her. Standing before them, she bowed her head slowly and smiled.

"Hello," she greeted them.

They remained silent. Matthew walked over and placed his hand upon the large bump on her abdomen. He chuckled slightly when he felt movement within.

"I feel him," Matthew whispered and looked up at Jeremy. "I'm sorry I doubted you."

"It's okay," Jeremy replied and looked at the others. "I don't know what happened with time. All I know is... this baby will be born in three months."

His friends nodded their heads slightly and walked toward Jade as well. Amber; however, remained standing by the silver fountain. Jeremy looked over at her and then immediately at Matthew.

"You brought Amber Drayke?!" he yelled at him in a whisper.

"Yes," Matthew answered. "When we got back, she saw us. Then, she started to glow like Sheila did. Well, we figured we'd bring her... maybe Jade can tell us who she is."

Jade looked over at Matthew when he mentioned her name. She then glanced over at the little girl, standing alone in the middle of the room.

"Who is she?" Jade asked, continuing to look at Amber.

"She's a neighborhood girl," Eddie answered. "We think she's a Triad, too."

Jade chuckled slightly and looked at Eddie. "What would make you think that?" she asked him.

"She started to glow... like you did on your throne, and like Sheila did after Shane hurt her," he answered.

Jade nodded her head and motioned for Amber to approach her. Reluctantly, Amber complied, and walked over to her.

"Hi," Jade whispered and knelt down to face her. "What is your name?"

"Amber," she replied and stared at Jade's enlarged abdomen.

Jade smiled and looked down at her abdomen as well. "Are you looking at my baby?" she asked her.

Amber nodded her head and said, "yes."

"He is going to grow up strong, and powerful," Jade told her. "That is his destiny."

"Isn't that unfair?" Amber asked her.

"Is what unfair?" Jade asked.

"Giving your baby a destiny before he is born," Amber answered.

The others looked over at Amber and Jade. Matthew scoffed and approached them. Jade looked up at him and shrugged her shoulders.

"Amber?" he asked, kneeling down beside Jade to face the little girl. "What are you talking about?"

"Your baby should be what he wants to be... not what someone tells him he should be," Amber said to Jade and flashed Matthew a crooked smile.

Matthew stood up and looked at his friends. He shook his head and walked away from Jade and Amber.

"That is one strange little girl," he whispered to Jeremy, standing at his side.

Jeremy led Matthew outside of the castle. He showed him the remodeling that he and Jade had made to the castle and outside structures.

"So, you're the king now, huh?" Matthew asked him, walking at his side.

"Yeah," Jeremy replied. "I really had to grow up."

"I see," Matthew said and stopped walking. Jeremy stopped and turned to his brother. "I really am sorry about that argument," Matthew told him and looked down.

"I'm over it," Jeremy replied and hugged him. "It's really great to see you."

"You, too," Matthew said and sighed. "By the way," he began and released his grip from Jeremy. "Happy belated birthday."

"What?" Jeremy asked, looking in his face.

"We missed our birthday," Matthew replied.

"So, we're sixteen now, huh?" he asked, smiling.

"Yeah, too bad we'll never get to drive," Matthew said and shook his head.

Jade decided to show the others around the castle. She led them to a room on the other side of the castle. Opening the doors, she walked through and showed them a magnificent room.

"This is where Jeremy and I hold meetings," she informed them.

Eddie, Sheila, and Amber gazed around the room in awe. At the back of the room sat two glistening thrones made of pure gold. A square table was stationary in the middle of the room with a dozen chairs positioned evenly around. The walls were covered with specs of gold, glittering from the light seeping in from the windows.

"We waited for you to arrive before we were married," Jade reminded them.

"Time seems to be screwed up," Eddie said and walked over to the thrones.

"I don't understand it," Sheila spoke and looked out the window. "We were only gone from here about six hours."

"I do not understand it, either," Jade said and sat down in one of the chairs.

"What's worse is that we can never go back home," Sheila said and turned around from the window. "The cops think Eddie murdered Shane… and Matthew and I were accomplices."

"They also think that something happened to Jeremy," Eddie added.

"That is horrible," Jade said and shook her head.

"Jade," Eddie began and approached her. Sitting down beside her, he said, "we brought the little girl with us for a purpose."

Jade looked over at Amber, standing in front of Jeremy's throne. "What is the purpose?" she asked Eddie.

"We think she is a Triad," he answered. "Is that possible?"

"No," Jade answered and looked into his face. "Sheila and my father are all that is left of the Triadal race."

"But she was glowing!" Eddie said and looked over at Amber. "There is something not right with her."

"She cannot be a Triad," Jade told him and sighed. "Unfortunately."

"Then, what is she?" Sheila asked, walking over to the table.

"She is just a little girl," Jade answered.

That evening, the friends gathered in the dining hall for dinner. Jade sat at the head of the table, while Jeremy sat at the foot. The others sat throughout and talked. All of a sudden, the dining hall door opened. The friends looked over and waited to see who would emerge. A moment passed with no one entering through the door. Eddie looked up at Jade, who remained sitting in her chair, unbothered.

He then looked back at the door. Again, nothing happened. Jeremy sighed and smiled at Jade, sitting across the long table from him.

"Uh," Eddie began. "Does it not bother anyone that the door just opened by itself?" he asked his friends.

"It bothers me," Matthew spoke out, looking at the door as well.

Just then, something grabbed Eddie's shoulder. Immediately, he screamed and jumped out of his seat. The others watched in horror as Eddie flailed his arms around, trying to hit his perpetrator.

"Eddie! It's alright!" Jeremy called out, standing to his feet.

"The hell it is!" Eddie yelled, continuing to flail his arms about.

Jeremy reached his arm out and touched Eddie on the shoulder. Eddie's attempts to strike the mystery intruder ceased as he looked into Jeremy's calm blue eyes.

"It's okay," Jeremy repeated and looked at the others.

Eddie struggled to catch his breath while Jeremy nodded his head to him. He pulled out Eddie's chair and invited him to take a seat. Eddie slowly sat down, looking around him for a sign of the entity.

"We have invited an old friend to hold the rank of general in our army," Jeremy explained to his friends, standing at the foot of the table. "General Reet Calhausen."

The teenagers gasped and looked around for their friend. "Where is he?" Sheila finally asked.

"I am here," Reet spoke out from behind Eddie.

Eddie immediately turned around to look at nothingness. Matthew and Sheila stood to their feet and approached Eddie's side of the table.

"Reet?" Sheila called out.

"Hello, Sheila," Reet answered.

Sheila gasped in delight when she felt a pair of warm arms wrap around her. She held out her arms and embraced Reet as well.

"He's still invisible, huh?" Matthew whispered to Jeremy.

"Yes," he answered. "We're unable to find a cure as of yet."

"Oh," Matthew said and looked down. "That's a shame."

"Not really," Reet's said. "I am the only invisible general in existence."

The others were silent.

"You don't understand?" Reet asked them and sighed. "No one can ever see me coming at them in a battle. I can lead from the front lines… and no one would ever know."

"I see," Matthew spoke and chuckled. "Ingenious."

"I thought so, too," Jeremy added. "But… there's more."

"More?" Eddie asked him, standing to his feet.

"Yes," he replied. "Jade and I have an army of hundreds."

"Have you been threatened?" Sheila asked, approaching him.

"Not yet," he answered. "But, it's inevitable. We have the Black Onyx… and when word gets out about this, they'll be coming from everywhere to fight for it."

"Well," Eddie began and smiled. "You have four more soldiers to add to your army."

Jeremy smiled and said, "I know. I couldn't be happier"

"Wait!" Matthew yelled out and faced his brother. "I'm not staying!"

"Wh-what do you mean you're not staying? If you go back… well, you know what will happen if you go back," Eddie told him.

"I don't care about that," Matthew said and shook his head. "I am done with fighting and meeting weird creatures and whatnot. I'm done."

"Are you sure about that?" Jeremy asked him quietly.

"Absolutely," Matthew answered. "It's been real fun but I just want to be normal for the remainder of my life. I mean… we missed our birthday, Jeremy! And I cannot quit thinking about what this is doing to Mom. She's miserable, if you didn't already know."

"I know it," Jeremy replied.

"Then, will you quit playing medieval times and come home with me?" Matthew asked him.

"No, I won't," he answered. "You knew the answer to that before you even asked."

"Guys," Sheila interrupted. "Please don't start with this again."

Matthew scoffed and looked away from Jeremy, while he shook his head and looked over at Jade.

Just then, two male Pixadairian soldiers walked through the door to the dining hall and approached Jade.

"Your Majesty," the first soldier spoke out to her. "There has been a breach in our border."

"What?" she asked quietly. She immediately looked over at Jeremy. "They have returned."

"Where?" Jeremy asked the Pixadairian soldier.

"Outer rim, Your Majesty," he answered. "Three unidentified aircraft."

"What's going on?" Eddie interrupted.

"Twice in the past month, intruders have made it across the border to Artobealu," Jeremy replied and quickly walked over to the window of the dining hall. "We were able to deter any invasion… but they shouldn't have returned so soon."

"I thought you said you weren't threatened?" Matthew asked, joining Jeremy at his side.

"They didn't threaten us," he answered.

Jade joined them as well and gazed out the window, searching for signs of threatening terrorists. She lowered her head and turned toward the Pixadairian soldiers.

"Colonel Hexum, you and Major Ciero organize a small group of militants and search the surrounding area," she ordered.

The two soldiers nodded their heads and rushed out the door. She sighed deeply and grabbed Jeremy's hand. Looking at the worried teenagers, she smiled softly and nodded her head.

"What should I do, Your Majesty?" Reet asked her.

"You will protect our friends at all costs," she instructed.

"I will," he complied.

Sheila gently took Amber's hand and walked across the room to join Jade and Jeremy. "Maybe we should take Amber somewhere else. She's just a little girl… and shouldn't be exposed to any kind of violence," she suggested.

"Great idea," Eddie agreed and looked at Jeremy. "Where can we hide her?" he asked him.

"We have a bunker set up underneath the castle," he answered and turned toward Jade. "You should go, too," he instructed her.

Jade scoffed quietly and shook her head. "Very well," she whispered and walked over to Amber. She took her hand and said, "I will take you there."

As Jade led Amber to the door, the little girl slowly looked back at the teenagers standing by the window, watching her leave. She waved to them as she walked out the door.

"That was a good idea," Jeremy told Sheila. "Jade shouldn't be out here, either."

"I agree with that," Eddie said and turned to the window. "Now, who are these guys?"

"We're not sure," Jeremy answered, turning toward the window as well. "We're not sure if they're friendly or hostile. All we know is that when they see our people approach, they scatter… and then they disappear."

"Disappear?" Matthew scoffed.

"Yeah! I know how it sounds… but that's what has happened," Jeremy answered.

"Alright… what do you want us to do?" Eddie asked him.

"We wait for news from the Colonel," he replied.

Amber held onto Jade's hand tightly while she led her to the bunker at the foundation of the castle. Her yellowish-brown eyes scanned the interior of the bunker. The huge room was filled with various supplies that would last years. A half dozen rolling cots were stationary at the rear of the bunker with blankets and pillows stacked neatly in the middle of each.

"Were you planning for the end of the world?" Amber asked Jade quietly.

"You can never be sure," she answered and sat down on one of the middle cots.

Amber shook her head slowly and examined the food supplies resting on hundreds of shelves stacked to the top of the room.

"Is your world threatened… or not?" Amber asked, turning toward Jade.

"It is not Artobealu that is threatened... it is me," she answered her.

"You?"

"Yes. I have something that everyone would want," she answered her and took a deep breath. "This item can make dreams come true."

"Is it the Black Onyx? I heard the others talking about it," Amber said and sat down on the cot next to Jade.

"Yes, it is," she replied.

"What does it do?" Amber asked her, placing her elbows on her knees and anxiously waiting for the answer.

"It can make anyone invincible," she answered.

"So they couldn't die?"

"Exactly. And that is exactly why everyone wants it."

"Oh," Amber said and looked down at her hands. "Jade… can I ask you something?"

"Sure," she invited.

"Why did I glow?"

"Why did you glow?" Jade asked, surprised by her question.

"Yes," Amber replied. "I shouldn't have been glowing… it doesn't make sense."

Jade chuckled nervously and inched back on the cot. "How does it not make sense?"

"Oh," Amber spoke when she noticed Jade's nervousness. "Please… don't be nervous. I'm harmless, really."

"Who are you?" Jade asked, standing to her feet.

"I am someone you never expected to see again," Amber answered and smiled.

Jeremy and his friends remained in the dining hall, waiting impatiently for news of the intruders. Eddie sat down in the chair that had been previously occupied by Jade, while Sheila and Matthew gazed out the window. Jeremy sighed deeply and sat down in the chair next to Eddie.

"I'm really sorry that you went through all that… you know, back home," Jeremy said to him.

"It's cool," Eddie replied. "We couldn't tell the truth no matter what. No one would believe us."

"Um… well, do you guys still have powers?" Jeremy asked, looking at Sheila and Matthew at the window.

"You know… to tell you the truth… we haven't even tried," Eddie said and chuckled. "I imagine so, since it's only been a few hours since we fought Shane."

"You gotta remember that time is messed up here, Eddie," Jeremy reminded him. "Maybe you should try."

"Okay," Eddie agreed and stood to his feet.

He placed his hands under the tabletop and employed his muscles to lift the table from the floor. Effortlessly, the four hundred pound table lifted from the floor on Eddie's end.

"I guess that answers my question, then," Jeremy said and chuckled.

"Matthew?" Eddie called out, catching his breath. "Maybe you ought to try."

"Alright," Matthew said and held out his arm.

His friends laughed in delight as the frosty wind surrounded him. Matthew chuckled as well, feeling the bitter cold from the cyclone splash his face.

"What abut Sheila?" Jeremy asked, turning toward her.

"She's okay," Eddie answered him. "We made it back, didn't we?"

"Right," Jeremy said and smiled.

At that moment, the same Pixadairian soldiers ran through the door and approached Jeremy. Both soldiers were identical clones, as Queen Xoula had explained to the teenagers before, but Jeremy had enforced the use of different color clothing in order to determine the difference between ranks. The colonel was dressed in dark blue, whereas the major was dressed in dark red. The subordinates were dressed in brown, so that they were able to blend in better with the plant life in Artobealu.

"Your Majesty," the colonel spoke, attempting to catch his breath. "We have lost them once again."

"You found nothing?" Jeremy asked, standing to his feet.

"Nothing at all, Sir," he replied.

"Very well," Jeremy said and sighed. "I want to introduce you to some very special friends of mine. They are going to be very essential to our army."

"Yes, King," the colonel said and bowed his head.

"This is Eddie Miles," Jeremy started and pointed to Eddie to his left. "Eddie, this is Colonel Hull Hexum, and Major Boone Ciero," Jeremy said.

Eddie reached his hand out to shake their hands. Instead of returning the gesture, the Pixadairian officers looked at him in confusion.

"Sorry, Eddie," Jeremy said and chuckled. "They're not familiar with hand shaking."

"Oh! That's no problem," Eddie said. "It's nice to meet you, anyway."

"And you, Eddie Miles," Colonel Hexum replied.

"Hull, Boone… this is Sheila Greise," Jeremy introduced her.

Hull and Boone turned to her and bowed their heads. Sheila smiled and bowed her head as well.

"Nice to meet you," Sheila said to them.

"You as well," Boone said and smiled at her.

"And, this is my brother, Matthew Germaine," Jeremy said, placing his arm around his shoulder.

"So, you guys are officers in the army, huh?" Matthew asked them.

"Yes," Hull answered.

"So, was either of you involved with the 'friendly' greeting we received when we were forced to land here?" Matthew asked them sarcastically.

"Matt," Jeremy said quietly.

"No, I want to know," Matthew said and looked at the identical Pixadairians.

"We both were," Hull answered him. "I was the personal guard to Queen Xoula."

"Interesting," Matthew said and scoffed. "You were the one that stood there and watched her die?"

"Yes," he replied.

"So, do you plan on giving Jade the same courtesy?" he asked him.

"I was given very specific orders," Hull justified.

"She told you to let her die?" Matthew scoffed.

"Yes," he answered.

"Look, Matthew," Jeremy interrupted. "Hull and Boone are the best soldiers on Artobealu… otherwise they would not hold rank."

"Whatever, Jeremy," Matthew said and turned away from him. "You just remember that when they stand by and watch Jade die."

THREE

UNINVITED

The teenagers, along with the Pixadairian soldiers, walked through the halls of the castle. Jeremy, ahead of the rest, nervously peered through each window he passed, watching for any sign of the intruders.

"What are we doing?" Matthew asked, joining him by his side.

"I don't have a good feeling about this," Jeremy answered.

"I would hope not," Matthew scoffed. "Strange creatures land in your world and just... disappear. I would agree that something is not right with that."

Jeremy opened the front door of the castle and led his friends outside. Instantly, they heard the same screeching noises that Eddie, Matthew, Sheila, and Amber heard when they arrived.

"What is that?" Jeremy asked, looking around in a panic.

"That is the noise they make," Boone answered. "It seems to be getting louder by the minute."

"That is because there are more and more arriving," Reet told them. "They're gathering together... for an invasion."

"Well," Eddie spoke and cracked his knuckles. "It's a good thing we arrived when we did, then."

"Your Majesty," Reet suddenly addressed Jeremy. "I suggest that you go back inside, now. I will venture into the forest alone to find out what they are."

Jeremy was silent. He looked out to the forest once again and sighed. "Alright, Reet. I guess that is the best idea," he told him.

"Okay," Reet spoke.

The teenagers listened as Reet's footsteps grew fainter as he departed. Eddie and Sheila walked through the castle door first, followed by Boone. Jeremy remained stationary, staring out into the direction of the screeching sounds. Matthew walked toward him and stood by his side.

"What's wrong? Well, besides the obvious," Matthew asked him.

Jeremy sighed deeply and said, "I just… I've never been in the position to lead people into battle, you know? I never thought that I was fit to be a king. But, now I am one… and I haven't the slightest clue what to do."

"Is that all?" Matthew asked and chuckled.

"Uh… that's a lot to be worried about," Jeremy said, facing him.

"Look, Eddie's here now. Look how much he's changed, you know? It's no problem… he'll be right there with you, every step of the way."

"I shouldn't have to depend on someone else," Jeremy said and turned to walk through the front door of the castle.

"You're not depending on him, Jeremy. We're here for support," Matthew said and patted him on the back. "It will be fine… it's not like this is our first battle or anything."

Jeremy nodded his head slowly and smiled at his brother. They approached Hull, who was standing guard at the castle entrance.

"Stand guard until General Calhausen returns," Jeremy ordered.

"Yes, Your Majesty," Hull replied.

Before Jeremy and Matthew could enter the castle; however, Reet yelled out to them, trying to catch his breath from running.

"Your Majesty!" he yelled.

"Reet?" Jeremy asked, standing in the doorway of the castle.

"Your Majesty," Reet said, trying to catch his breath. "You wouldn't believe…"

"Take your time," Jeremy said, reaching out to place his hand on Reet's shoulder.

Eddie, Sheila, and Boone then walked through the door to join the others.

"What's going on?" Sheila asked them.

"Reet's back," Matthew answered her.

"There are thousands… thousands of them," Reet explained. "And they've been here the whole time!"

"What do you mean they've been here the whole time?" Jeremy asked.

"They never disappeared!" Reet replied. "They've been collecting an army… all this time!"

"Reet, calm down and tell me what you saw," Jeremy said quietly.

"Wait," Eddie interrupted. "Maybe it would be best if we went inside, huh?"

"Right," Jeremy said and nodded his head.

Hull and Boone led the teenagers through the door and into a small room to the right of the entrance. Boone watched through the small window in the room, while Hull stood guard at the door.

"Finish what you were saying," Jeremy ordered to Reet.

"Okay," Reet started, breathing heavily. "They're the same size as us… but… they can shrink instantly. That's how they were able to disappear when our soldiers approached them. But, they didn't actually disappear."

"How do you know that?" Eddie asked him.

"Because… I accidentally stepped on one," Reet answered.

The teenagers were silent. They merely looked in the direction of Reet's voice, completely bewildered by what he was telling them.

"Okay," Matthew finally said. "How do we handle this situation?"

"Not sure," Reet replied. "When they shrink, they're the size of a thumb… if that. Oh… and they blend in with the forest floor as well."

"Great! All we have to do is step on them! Okay, problem solved," Matthew said and walked to the door. "Well, come on! We've got some critter stomping to do!"

"Matthew… you're missing the point," Reet said.

Matthew stopped and turned toward Reet's voice. "What point?" he asked.

"If they can shrink... then they can return to their normal size," he explained.

Matthew looked down at the grounds and groaned. "That certainly changes things," he said and shook his head.

"Look, we need to come up with a plan," Eddie said and stood in front of Jeremy. "You have an army of hundreds, right?" he asked him.

"Yeah," Jeremy answered. "But, there's no way we can win against an army of thousands... of... whatever they are," he said and pointed to the window.

"Let me worry about that," Eddie said and smiled.

Eddie, Matthew, Sheila, and Jeremy stood outside in front of the door of the castle, nervously awaiting word from Colonel Hexum and Major Ciero, who had been ordered to gather the Pixadairian army.

"I don't like this," Sheila said and sighed. "They've been gone too long."

"Sheila, it takes a while to gather an army of hundreds," Matthew said and snickered. "They'll be here."

"Jeremy," Eddie spoke and turned to him. "Do you trust Hull and Boone?"

"Of course I do," Jeremy answered and chuckled. "Why would you ask that?"

"Well, I was just thinking... what if Matthew was right? He made a good point about Hull leaving Queen Xoula to die."

"I would rather have a Colonel willing to follow orders, even if it meant that he would have to witness Jade's death," Jeremy replied. "Colonel Hexum was ordered by Queen Xoula to leave her be. So, he did."

"I don't know," Eddie said and sighed. "Why would Queen Xoula order that? It doesn't make sense."

"Well-," Jeremy began before he caught a glimpse of Colonel Hexum and Major Ciero approaching them.

"Your Majesty," Hull spoke, out of breath. "The army has been assembled. General Calhausen is standing by for orders."

"Good," Jeremy replied. "You and Major Ciero go to the bunker and bring Jade and Amber up here."

"Yes, Sir," Hull complied. He and Boone then walked away to gather the queen and young girl from the bunker below the castle.

"What? Why?" Sheila asked Jeremy as the Pixadairian soldiers departed.

"Trust us," Eddie interrupted and smiled at her.

Suddenly, the teenagers were started by the sounds of screaming, growing closer to them. Eddie immediately pushed Sheila behind him, while Matthew and Jeremy began to produce their powers.

Jeremy's hand filled with flowing water as Matthew's body became engulfed with bitter frost. The two brothers then stood in front of Eddie and waited for something to appear from within the forest ahead of them.

Then, without warning, a woman appeared, running at high speed toward the confused teenagers. Her screaming ceased when she caught sight of them, but she continued running toward them.

"Stop there!" Jeremy yelled out to her, raising his hand with the water flowing abundantly.

"She's not one of yours?" Matthew asked him.

"No," he replied. "I've never seen her before."

The frightened woman ignored Jeremy's warning and continued to run for them. Jeremy hesitated at first, but then began to push the water from his palm, aiming at the woman.

"Stop!" Sheila yelled out at Jeremy and pulled his arm down.

The stream of water from his palm penetrated the ground without his control. He gasped and attempted to stop pushing the water outward, but could not.

"Sheila!" he yelled at her, as he finally stopped the water from flowing.

The cyclone of icy cold wind blew away as Matthew stopped invoking his power, and attempted to assist his brother.

The terrified woman finally reached the teenagers and collapsed. Eddie quickly caught her before she fell to the ground. He gently picked her up and walked into the castle.

"What are you doing?" Jeremy called out to Eddie.

"Let him," Sheila said to Jeremy and followed Eddie into the castle.

"What is this? Do I not have a say? I mean, it's only *my* world," Jeremy said to Matthew, who remained standing at his side.

"Don't start with that," Matthew replied and walked through the castle door as well.

He walked down the hall, following the sounds of gasps and cries from the strange woman. The echoing sounds led him to the last room on the left. He slowly opened the door and saw the woman lying on the bed with Sheila at her side, holding her hand. Eddie turned around to Matthew and shrugged his shoulders.

"Who is she?" Matthew asked Eddie, joining him by his side.

"Not sure," he answered him.

"Hey," Sheila whispered to her friends. "Maybe we should have a minute, huh?"

"Oh, yeah," Eddie replied and walked to the door. "Come on, Matthew," he suggested and opened the door.

"Right," Matthew said and walked through the door. He walked into the hall and faced his brother.

"I'm sorry," Jeremy spoke as they faced him. "With all that's going on… I thought she was the enemy."

"A frightened woman… screaming and running *away* from whatever's in the forest… is the enemy?" Matthew said and scoffed. "Right, Jeremy."

"I didn't think," Jeremy whispered and looked down.

"It's okay," Eddie said and patted Jeremy on the back. "It's done and forgotten about."

"It's just… I have Jade, and… the Pixadairians depend on me… I didn't think," Jeremy said quietly.

"I would have done the same thing," Eddie said and smiled at him.

Sheila finally emerged from the room and inhaled deeply. She wore a look of shock and dismay on her face. Eddie stood to his feet and looked at her.

"So?" he asked her quietly.

"I think you guys need to hear this," she replied and swallowed hard. "But, not from me."

"What… what is it?" Jeremy asked, standing to his feet as well.

"Sheila?" Matthew whispered, taking a step closer to her.

Sheila sighed deeply and blinked her eyes several times, trying to accept what she had been told by the strange young woman.

"Uh… you're scaring me a little," Matthew told her in a whisper.

"I'm… I'm terrified," she spoke slowly and lowered her head. "Go… go and speak with her."

"Are you sure?" Jeremy asked.

"Yes," she replied and raised her hands to cover her eyes. "You need to hear it."

Eddie, Matthew, and Jeremy looked at one another in fear. They had never witnessed Sheila acting as peculiar as she had at that moment.

"After you," Matthew said to Eddie and pointed to the door.

Eddie nodded his head slowly and reached for the doorknob. He turned it and pushed the door open. Very slowly, he entered the room and looked at the woman, sitting straight up in the bed, staring at him.

Matthew walked through next, followed by Jeremy. They slowly approached the young woman and stood at the bedside, keeping their eyes on her.

She was dressed in a white gown, with multiple grass stains imprinted into the fabric. Her long, unkempt hair was light blonde in color, and filled with twigs and branches from the forest floor. Her gray eyes portrayed terror and hopelessness with a hint of rage as she looked at the teenage boys.

"Can you tell us your name?" Eddie quietly asked her.

The woman slowly raised her hands to her round face and pushed the hair behind her ears. She sighed deeply and looked at Eddie intensely. He sensed her sudden rage and backed away from the bed. Matthew and Jeremy each took a step back as well, keeping their eyes fixed on her.

"I am not the one you should fear," she spoke up with a soft, pleasant voice.

"Oh?" Matthew asked her, swallowing hard.

"No," she replied. "I was taken from my home… by the Cembalotes."

"The... what?" Matthew asked her.

"Wait!" Eddie yelled out and stood in front of his friends. "That is what Queen Xoula said Shane was!"

"A Cembalote?" Jeremy asked and chuckled. "Are you sure?"

"Yeah! He's right!" Matthew said and looked at his brother. "That's the sub-breed of Pixadairie... I remember now!"

"That's all fine and good, but... what does that have to do with you?" Jeremy asked, focusing his attention on the woman.

"I am Velexia La Croix, but they call me Vexy," she replied and smiled at him. "*I* am a Cembalote."

The three teenagers stopped breathing and stared at the mysterious woman as she stood to her feet slowly. She sighed deeply and walked toward Jeremy. Nervously, he raised his hand to her and struggled to produce the flow of water in his shaky hand.

"You mustn't do that," she warned him and gently placed her hand upon his forearm. "I am aware that you are the king of Artobealu. So, I must speak with you... and *only* you."

"N-no," he replied, his voice shaky. "Whatever you have to say to me... you can say to my friends."

Matthew and Eddie approached the tormented Cembalote and stood at Jeremy's side.

"Very well," she said and removed her hand from Jeremy. Turning away from them, she walked to the window in the room and peered out. "I was taken from my home and forced to join an army of thousands," she began. "An army of those like me; the Cembalotes."

Eddie, Matthew, and Jeremy remained standing stationary in the middle of the room, listening carefully to every word she spoke.

"I do not like war, you see. I refused to fight. I did not want to be involved in anything that would cause harm to others," she explained, weeping softly. "I had no choice."

"Is that what is out there in the forest? Cembalotes?" Jeremy asked her, taking a step forward.

"Yes," she answered. "We have been collecting thousands for a while now."

"Reet was right," Jeremy whispered and raised his hand to his mouth.

"Why are you here?" Eddie asked her.

"We are here for one reason... a stone," she replied.

"I knew it!" Matthew shouted and raised his hands in the air. "We shouldn't have come back here!"

"Matt! Now's not the time!" Jeremy yelled.

"Vexy," Eddie started and walked toward her. "How do you know of this stone?"

"Our leader," she answered him. "The infinite one."

As those words left her lips, Eddie fell to his knees, Matthew's jaw opened in shock, and Jeremy merely stared at her.

"You know of him?" she asked them.

The three were silent.

Vexy shook her head in confusion at the boys' sudden change in behavior. She walked to Jeremy and looked into his bright blue eyes.

"He is very dangerous," she whispered to him. "*Very* dangerous."

Jeremy nodded his head and turned to the door. "Vexy, you just stay here a moment, okay?" he ordered. "Matthew, Eddie... I need to speak with you both," he said, turning his focus to his perplexed friends.

The three walked out of the room and into the hallway to join Sheila. She was sitting on the floor with her back against the wall and her hands covering her forehead. Eddie walked to her and sat down beside her. Gently, he took her hand, holding it in his.

"Okay, guys," Jeremy addressed them. "I don't know how this is possible, but apparently it is."

"Shane is dead!" Matthew yelled, turning his back to them, raising his hand to his head. "We all saw him die!"

"Actually," Eddie quietly spoke. "We didn't actually *see* him die. We turned away... remember?"

Matthew became silent, scanning his memory for that exact moment when Shane plummeted to the ground.

"Wait, guys," Sheila said, looking up at the twins. "Do you realize what this means? Shane has come for the Black Onyx... and this time... he has an army of shrinking soldiers. They could be in the castle now for all we know!"

"No, we would know," Jeremy said, disagreeing with her.

"How would you? Reet said they can shrink to the size of a thumb!" she retorted.

"Just forget that for a minute," Eddie said and exhaled. "What's our next move?"

"I haven't the faintest idea," Jeremy answered.

"Wait!" Matthew said and raised his hand. "How do we know we can trust *her*?" he whispered, pointing to the room where Vexy was.

"He's got a point," Jeremy agreed.

"Did you guys see her? She was terrified! I highly doubt that she is with them," Sheila disputed.

"I don't know… This has just been a really *weird* day," Matthew said and leaned against the wall.

Just then, Hull and Boone approached the teenagers, with Jade and Amber in tow. The four had not been advised of Vexy's sudden appearance, so they looked at the teenagers' sullen faces in perplexity.

"What is the matter, Your Highness?" Hull asked Jeremy, facing him.

"You wouldn't believe it," he answered and shook his head. His eyes then focused on Jade. Her face was damp with tears, and she wore a distraught look upon her face. Immediately, she ran to him.

"Oh, Jeremy! I must speak with you right away!" she pleaded, burying her face into his chest.

"Jade," Jeremy said quietly. "Now is really not the time."

Jade released her grip from him and looked up into his face. "What?" she asked.

"Um… we have some really big problems," he explained and sighed.

"But, I have to tell you something important," she whispered.

"Hey, guys!" Matthew abruptly shouted, pointing out the window of the hallway. "We're going to have company here… real quick."

"What is it?" Jeremy asked and immediately jogged to the window. He peered out and gasped quietly at the sight of thousands of human-like creatures approaching the castle.

"It's the Cembalotes!" Sheila yelled and ran to the door to alert Vexy.

"Wait!" Eddie ordered and placed himself between Sheila and the door. "We have to come up with a plan… quickly."

As the teenagers scrambled to concoct a successful plan, the army of Cembalotes reached the castle doors. The frightened door keeper quickly backed away from the door and fled the area, hoping to find safety within the many hiding places throughout the castle.

The determined mob of shrinking soldiers gathered at the door and awaited their orders. These marvelous creatures had blonde hair and gray eyes, similar to Shane and Vexy, but were not identical with one another. The males were dressed in white tunics and black trousers, while the females were dressed in long white gowns. Both male and female Cembalotes wore wide black belts at the waist, with weapons fastened at the side. The weapons varied from laser guns, swords, axes, knives, and sticks they had collected from the forest floor.

Anxiously, the army of Cembalotes stood at the door and prepared themselves for battle. Through the middle of the organized group, a young man made his way through. His heavy black boots kicked the rocks as he approached the front of the army. He was dressed in form fitting maroon slacks, a slim black belt at his waist, and a plain black tunic. His belt buckle reflected the light from the bright sky as he stood before his subordinates. It was Shane Aramay; alive and well and leading an army of his species.

"We will take back what is ours!" he addressed his peers.

The crowd of Cembalotes cheered, throwing their arms into the air. Shane chuckled and nodded his head to them. He ran his right hand through his short blonde hair and closed his eyes. Raising his left hand to the sky, he attempted to visualize what his former friends were doing at that very moment.

"Sir?" a male Cembalote spoke to Shane.

Shane slowly opened his eyes and sighed. Looking down at his colonel, he asked, "yes, Timothy?"

"Perhaps we should open the door?" he suggested.

"In due time," Shane replied. "Be patient."

The Cembalotes continued to stand at the door, waiting for the right moment to enter. Shane's colonel stood guard at the side of the castle. His hands shook nervously and sweat streamed down his face. Suddenly, he caught a glimpse of something moving in the bushes at the other end of the castle.

"Sir?" he called out to Shane.

Shane departed his anxious army and approached the colonel. "Yes, Timothy?"

"There's something moving over there," Timothy replied, pointing to the bushes.

Shane stood at his colonel's side and watched carefully, waiting to witness the same movement. Just then, Timothy and Shane watched as Eddie appeared from behind the bushes, followed by Vexy, Jeremy, and a pregnant Jade.

"Oh!" Shane said furiously and shook his head. "I didn't see that happening!"

Immediately, he turned around to return to his group of soldiers. Timothy, nervous and unsure about Shane's actions, jogged behind him. "What do we do?" he asked.

"We attack!" Shane yelled out to his army. "Now!"

Instantly, each Cembalote drew their weapon and yelled out in war cries. Shane, accompanied by his army of Cembalotes, walked steadily around the castle and in the direction of the fleeing teenagers.

"Get them! Now!" Shane ordered. "They have your stone!"

The Cembalotes at the front line ran full force toward an airship in the middle of the landing strip at the side of the castle. The side doors on the airship then began to close, as the engines ignited.

Shane ceased walking and watched as his army finally reached the airship. The angry mob pounded on the sides of the airship, warning the occupants of their intentions.

Shane watched in anger as the occupants in the airship ignored their attackers and revved the airship's engines, preparing to depart Artobealu. Shane's colonel then joined him at his side and watched the airship begin to elevate in the air, flying away.

"Sir? They're leaving," Timothy informed him.

"Yes, I know," Shane replied and turned to him. "Take a small group and follow them."

"Follow them, Sir?"

"Follow them, and get that damn stone!" Shane ordered. Shane turned from him and began to walk away. "Inform me as soon as you have it!"

Timothy sighed deeply and complied with his orders. He gathered a small group of strong soldiers and walked quickly to the nearest airship.

Shane; however, approached the castle. His face burned with anger as he clinched his fists in rage. To his utter surprise, he watched as hundreds of Pixadairian soldiers ran toward him and his army.

Quickly, he turned around to his unsuspecting army to see if they had taken notice of their surprise attackers.

"Attack!" Shane called out to his army.

The Cembalotes immediately turned their attention away from the departing aircraft and to the group of creatures, desperate to protect their land.

As the Pixadairian soldiers approached him, Shane raised his hands toward them, and enlisted one of his many powers. Orbs of red flaming fire formed in his right palm, and he unemotionally thrust flames at several of the soldiers. He then began to walk toward the castle as his countless victims screamed loudly in agony and rolled upon the ground, desperate to douse the flames.

Turning around, he watched his army of Cembalotes battle the Pixadairians. It was obvious to him that the Pixadairians were outnumbered, and stood at a disadvantage. Their only defense against the massively shrinking soldiers was their levitation ability, which in this case did not assist them much. Shane's Cembalotes fought brutally again their opponents; decreasing their size, stealthily approaching a victim, and returning to normal size before the Pixadairie soldier had a chance to realize what had happened. They used this tactic to quickly run their various weapons though the unsuspecting natives, striking them down. The undeniable sounds of weapons clashing and bodies falling were heard throughout the land as the horrid battle continued.

"That's what they get," Shane spoke to himself and chuckled.

He then turned around and continued approaching the castle. Suddenly, he caught sight of a very young Pixadairian male, alone and terrified, with his back against the castle, clinching his weapon tightly.

"You got somewhere you have to be?" Shane asked the young male.

The Pixadairian soldier breathed heavily in a panic and nodded his head quickly. Shane chuckled and walked toward him. The young soldier shook in fear and raised his sword closer to himself.

"What's your name?" Shane asked, standing in front of him.

"Kibtelo," the soldier answered.

"You got a last name, boy?" Shane asked, chuckling.

The young male nodded his head and answered, "Cal-Calhausen."

FOUR

Deception

The airship sped into the air at full force, departing Artobealu. Eddie quickly approached the front of the plane and looked down at the empty pilot's seat. He sighed deeply and said, "I think we did it, Reet."

"We can only hope that it worked," Reet replied from the pilot's chair.

"I saw a group of Cembalotes load one of your airships," Eddie said and sat down in the co-pilot's seat. "I think they're following us."

"Then your plan was successful," Reet said. "The stone will remain safe."

"I just hope Jeremy, Jade, and Amber stay safe," he replied and leaned back in the chair.

"I'll have you know that this is not too entirely comfortable," Sheila said as she approached the front of the plane. She rolled her eyes and removed the pillow from underneath the bright green gown she had taken from Jade.

"Sheila!" Eddie yelled and grabbed the pillow from her hands. "You have to keep this!"

Sheila groaned and took the pillow from him. She pulled the hood of the robe down from her head and ran her hands through her long dark hair. "I thought the deception was over."

"It won't be over for a long time," Matthew said, walking toward her. He was wearing Jeremy's clothes, and atop his head, sat Jeremy's shimmering crown. "That was a pretty good idea, by the way," Matthew said, addressing Eddie. "Using mine and Jeremy's identical features to our advantage."

"I knew it would work," Eddie said and chuckled.

"Uh, maybe too well," Reet said from the pilot's chair. "We're being followed."

"Don't worry, Reet," Eddie said and looked out the window at the airship following behind. "That's precisely what we wanted."

"Well, what do we do now?" Sheila asked him, covering her head with the hood once again.

"We have to lead them as far from Artobealu as possible," Eddie answered her.

"Eddie," Matthew began and looked out the window as well. "That's just *one* airship. There were thousands of soldiers… they couldn't all fit in there."

"Remember," Vexy spoke, walking toward the front. "We can shrink."

"Ah!" Matthew said and chuckled. "Brilliant."

Shane smiled at the young Pixadairie and turned his head to watch the brutal battle continue between the species. "I'm Shane," he said quietly.

The young male nodded his head slowly and glanced over at the battle as well. Carefully, he took a step away from Shane.

"What are you doing out here?" Shane asked the frightened youngster, turning to him.

"I- I wanted… I wanted to help," he answered nervously.

"How old are you?" Shane asked him, taking a step closer.

"I'm ten," he replied and looked down at the ground.

"Ten? Jeez… that's awful young to be out here in all this mess, don't you think?"

Kibtelo nodded his head and turned his attention over to the field, watching in sorrow as his people were being defeated.

"Do you know your way inside the castle?" Shane asked, slowly pulling his hand behind his back.

The young male swallowed hard as he noticed Shane taking another step closer to him, concealing his hand behind his back.

"Y- yes," he whispered, keeping his focus on Shane's movements.

"Good!" Shane exclaimed and pulled his hand out from behind his back. He walked to Kibtelo's side and placed his arm around him. "Lucky for you."

Kiptelo's eyes widened while Shane looked into his face. "What are you… going to do?"

"You are going to take me on a tour," Shane answered him and encouraged him to walk forward.

As they approached the front door of the castle, Shane pointed to the door handle. Kibtelo took a deep breath and slowly opened the door. He led Shane through and into a long hallway.

"Where does this lead?" Shane asked him, taking hold of his arm.

"To the center on the castle," he replied.

"Let's go then," Shane said and chuckled. "I want to search every inch of this building… and you're coming with me."

"Wh- why do you need me?" Kibtelo asked, his voice shaking with fear.

Shane stopped walking and pulled Kibtelo's arm, causing him to turn to face him. Shane then bent down to look into the terrified male's eyes.

"I see something very special in you, boy," Shane answered. "If you cooperate… I will give you a very powerful gift. Would you like that?"

Kibtelo looked down, away from Shane and nodded his head. "What kind of gift?"

"A gift that I guarantee you will not be able to refuse," Shane whispered and smiled. "I have the ability to make you powerful… more powerful than you could ever imagine."

Kibtelo stopped breathing and looked into Shane's face once again. "I want to be powerful," he said and smiled slightly. "I want to make my father proud."

"So be it, then," Shane said and chuckled. "You help me… and I will help you. Deal?"

"Deal," Kibtelo agreed.

"We should lead them to Sua Deg," Reet suggested to Eddie.

"Why Sua Deg?" Eddie asked, turning around in the co-pilot's seat toward the empty pilot's chair.

"Think about what you consider to be true magic. Very powerful… completely unbelievable," Reet told him. "Well, the magic on Sua Deg is *nothing* like that. Nothing like you could ever imagine."

"That's… that's where that magician was from, right? The one that created the Triad's stones?" Matthew interrupted, leaning against the back of Eddie's chair.

"Yeah! Maz!" Eddie said and sat straight up. "He was from Sua Deg!"

"Well, as you can recall… Maz is no longer available," Matthew said and turned away, walking toward the rear of the aircraft.

He sighed deeply and sat down on the bench in the back of the aircraft next to Vexy. She looked over at him and smiled softly, pointing to the crown on his head.

"Astonishing," she spoke.

"What? The crown?" he asked and grabbed it from his head. He ran his hands through his dark hair and looked down at the magnificent sign of royalty in his hand. "I can't believe my brother is a king."

"I can," Vexy said and turned to face him. "He is very brave."

"Humph, he wasn't always like that," he said and chuckled. "He used to be a coward like the rest of us."

"You're not cowards," Vexy said and placed her hand on his. "You and your friends are *very* brave for what you have just done… to save your friends."

Matthew smiled slightly and looked at her. "You think?"

"Yes! Of course!"

"Yeah, well… he would have done the same thing," Matthew said and stood up. He walked to the side window of the ship and looked out at nothing but dark and empty space.

Vexy sighed and stood to her feet as well. She approached him and stood at his side, glancing out the window. "What is troubling you?" she asked him.

"I'm scared for him," he answered quietly.

"I am sure he will be fine," she assured him.

"I'm afraid that I will never see him again," he said and turned to her. "You know? Like… that was the last time that I will ever see my brother."

"What makes you think that?"

"It's just a… a weird feeling I get every once in a while," he answered and chuckled nervously. "It's probably nothing."

"What's the course heading?" Timothy asked the pilot in the airship following Eddie and his friends.

"Well, it appears as if they're heading to… Sua Deg," the pilot answered and looked up at his superior. "Why would they possibly want to go to there?"

"How would I know?" Timothy replied.

He turned away from the pilot and approached the small group of Cembalotes waiting in the rear of the plane. Standing before them, he raised his hand up, motioning that he wanted silence. His subordinates immediately ceased their chatting and turned their undivided attention to him.

"Our target is leading us to… Sua Deg," he addressed them.

Immediately, the group of Cembalotes gasped loudly and looked at one another in panic.

"No! No, Timothy!" a single male Cembalote shouted, standing to face him. "This has gone far enough! You have to stop this!"

"Sit, Mason," Timothy ordered.

"You have the authority… to stop this," Mason whispered to him. "Please… you must stop this. You must stop Shane."

"You need… to sit, Mason," Timothy ordered once again.

An additional Cembalote stood to his feet and looked into Timothy's face. "Timothy… Shane is leading us to certain death," the frightened Cembalote spoke. "Please, please… don't make us go to Sua Deg."

"I have my orders, Keilo, just as you have yours," Timothy said calmly and turned to approach the front of the aircraft.

"I won't do it, Timothy!" Keilo shouted. "I will not go to Sua Deg again!"

"You don't have a choice, Keilo," Timothy said quietly, continuing to walk away. "None of us do."

"Well, what do we have down here, Kib?" Shane asked the young Pixadairie as he looked into a dark room at the end of the hall.

"Storage," Kibtelo replied. "Just some stuff left over from… from Queen Xoula," he said and lowered his head.

Shane shut the door and looked over at him. "I'm guessing that you liked her?"

"Of course," he answered. "She was a good queen."

"Yeah… I wouldn't know," Shane said and chuckled.

Then, something caught Shane's attention. He turned and walked to the middle of the floor and knelt down. Carefully, he picked up a small gemstone from the floor and held it in his hands. Kibtelo approached him and examined the shiny green gem lying in the middle of Shane's hand.

"Oh, that's a stone from King Jeremy's crown," Kibtelo informed Shane.

"What?" Shane said and stood to his feet. "This is from Jeremy's crown?"

"Yeah," he answered.

Shane suddenly looked away from the boy and noticed an additional gemstone lying a few feet away. Quickly, he walked over and picked it up.

"And, this?" he asked, showing the stone to Kibtelo.

"Uh-huh," he replied, nodding his head.

"What kind of king… allows stones to fall from his crown… without replacing them?" Shane asked quietly to himself.

"Maybe he didn't know they fell out," Kibtelo suggested.

"Nah," Shane said and held the stones up. "This king would know."

Kibtelo stood in confusion as Shane placed the stones in his pocket. He placed his hand to his chin and slowly paced in a circle. Finally, he stopped and turned to the boy.

"Where would someone go… if the castle was under attack?" he asked him.

Kibtelo paused and looked down slightly. "Well… that would be the bunker… under the castle."

"Take me there," Shane ordered, smiling evilly at the young Pixadairie.

"We have to come up with a plan… quickly," Eddie said, blocking Sheila from the door.

"Well, what do you suggest we do?" Matthew asked, turning his attention to the approaching army of Cembalotes.

"There's nothing much we can do," Jeremy said and turned to Jade. "Whatever happens… I will not let harm come to you, or our baby."

"I know that," Jade said and smiled softly to him.

"Your Majesties… I suggest that we take you to safety," Hull said, walking to them. "And the little girl."

"She is not-" Jade started before she was interrupted by the sound of shouting Cembalotes from in front of the castle door.

"Quickly, Your Majesties," Boone said nervously, clinching his sword close to him.

"Wait! I've got it!" Eddie shouted and walked over to stand in front of Jeremy and Jade. "Jeremy, give Matthew your clothes and crown."

"What? Why?" Jeremy asked, perplexed at Eddie's odd request.

"The Cembalotes will think that Matthew is… you," he explained. "Meanwhile, we'll dress Sheila up to look like Jade."

"What purpose would that serve? You would just be putting Matthew and Sheila in danger," Jade said quietly. "I could not agree with that."

"No, listen… trust me, okay?" Eddie said and smiled. "Matthew, Sheila, and I will leave in one of your aircrafts and lead them away from here… so that you, Jeremy, and Amber will be safe."

"Lead them where? And what makes you think that they would follow you?" Jade asked him.

"Jade... Shane knows that you have the Black Onyx. Why else would he be here with a massive army?" Eddie replied.

"I do not like the idea of this," Jade said and looked down.

"I know you don't, Jade. You're a very stubborn person... But please... think about your baby," Eddie whispered.

"No! This plan is brilliant!" Matthew exclaimed and stood to face Jeremy. "Give me your crown, brother."

"No, I'm with Jade," Jeremy said. "I will never forgive myself if something happens to you."

"Don't worry about it," Matthew said and reached up to grab the crown from Jeremy's hand.

Instantly, Jeremy grabbed the crown as well. The others watched as the brothers each tugged at the crown, trying to take it from one another.

"Jeremy, I'm doing this for you!" Matthew shouted.

"I never asked you to!" Jeremy retorted and pulled the crown toward him.

"Guys, please! We don't have time for this!" Sheila yelled and grabbed the crown as well.

She tugged hard at the crown, causing the brothers to release their grips. Instantly, the crown flew from Sheila's grip and crashed against the wall in the hallway. Two gemstones flew from the crown and fell to the floor. Jeremy calmly walked over to the crown and picked it up from the floor. He looked down at the empty voids and sighed deeply.

"I'm sorry, Jeremy," Sheila whispered.

"It's okay, Sheila," Jeremy said quietly. "I shouldn't have been so stubborn." He then turned to Matthew and held the crown out for him.

"Jeremy, I'm sorry about your crown," Matthew said, taking his brother's sign of royalty from him. "But I care more about your life right now."

"I know, Matt," Jeremy said and looked into his brother's face. "It's just that... I care about your life too."

Matthew nodded his head and reached his arms out, pulling Jeremy close to him. The brothers continued to hug one another tightly while the Cembalotes continued to gather outside.

"So, what's this plan, Eddie? What exactly are we to do?" Jeremy asked him, releasing his grip on Matthew.

"Okay," Eddie said and stood in front of his friends. "We'll dress Matthew up to look exactly like you. It would fool anyone!"

"Not Shane," Jeremy said and shook his head. "He can tell the difference."

"Well... we'll be at a distance... so he would not know any different," Eddie suggested and turned to Sheila and Jade. "We're gonna need a pillow for you, Sheila," he addressed her.

She smiled and nodded her head. "I think this is a great plan, Eddie."

"It is a great plan, Eddie... but you forgot one important factor," Jade told him.

"What's that?" he asked.

"Who is going to fly the aircraft?" she asked and looked at the teenagers. "None of you know how to fly."

Eddie sighed and began to think of another plan. Then, the thought crossed his mind. "Reet!" he shouted. "Reet will fly! It's perfect! No one will even know that he is there!"

"Now, wait a minute," Jeremy started. "He's the general to the army, Eddie. We can't just pull him away."

"Your Majesty," Hull interrupted. "I would be honored to lead the army... in General Calhausen's absence."

"There you go, Jeremy! This plan will work!" Eddie said excitedly.

"Colonel Hexum, are you sure that you are prepared to lead an army into battle?" Jeremy asked him.

"I was born ready, Sir," he replied and turned to walk away. "I will have General Calhausen report back to you right away."

As Hull walked out of the castle at the rear entrance, Jeremy and Matthew decided to exchange clothes. They walked into the room across the hall from Vexy's, while Sheila and Jade walked into the room beside them.

Eddie, Amber, and Boone remained standing in the hallway. Boone continued to watch out the window for any sudden movement by the Cembalotes. Amber sat on the floor with her knees to her chest, and her head down. Eddie took notice to her, and sat down next to her.

"Everything's going to fine," he quietly told her. "Jeremy and Jade are going to take good care of you."

"I know that," she whispered and looked up at him.

"It'll be fine," he said and placed his hand on her shoulder. "They will not let anything happen to you."

"They are so lucky to have a friend like you," she said and smiled softly. "You are so brave."

"I wasn't before, you know," he said and chuckled. "I'm sure you remember that."

"Dirk and Chuck," Amber replied and nodded her head. "Of course I remember all that. You know, after you guys disappeared... they questioned those two."

"Really?" Eddie asked, surprised.

"Oh, yeah," she answered and laughed. "The cops thought they had something to do with it. You know, after they found out Dirk and Chuck were known as the neighborhood bullies and all."

"That's interesting," Eddie said and shook his head.

All of a sudden, Boone gasped and backed away from the window. He held his weapon out in front of him and leaned against the wall in the hallway. Eddie stood to his feet and approached him.

"Boone? What is it?" he asked, looking out the window.

"I don't know if I can do this," he replied. "There are so many of them... and so few of us."

"I know, Boone," Eddie said and looked at him. "It doesn't seem fair."

Just then, Jeremy and Matthew emerged from the room. Matthew was dressed in Jeremy's royal clothes, while Jeremy was wearing Matthew's clothes.

"I feel ridiculous," Matthew said, looking down at his pants and boots.

"Oh, no! You look like royalty," Eddie said and chuckled.

"Very funny," Matthew said and rolled his eyes. "Jeremy, I don't know how you could stand wearing all this crap."

"Umm... I picked that stuff out," Jeremy said and cleared his throat.

"Sorry," Matthew whispered and smiled.

"Eddie, how do you know this plan will work?" Jeremy asked him, looking out the window at the growing number of Cembalotes.

"I don't for sure," he answered. "I'm just going on a little faith."

"Well, I hate to break it to you, but we're going to need a lot more than faith. I mean, the Cembalotes outnumber the Pixadairies by thousands. You realize this, right?" Jeremy asked, turning away from the window.

"Of course," Eddie answered quietly.

"To be honest with you, I do not feel comfortable leaving my people to fight a battle... without me in front, leading them," he added.

"You'll be no good to them dead, Jeremy. Besides, you need to protect Jade and your baby. After all, he's going to grow up to lead many to victory… remember?" Eddie asked.

"Yes, I remember," Jeremy answered and looked back out the window. "But I don't want to desert my people."

"Jeremy, you won't be deserting them," Matthew told him, placing his hand on his shoulder. "Your son's well being is most important… you know? For victory."

"Alright," Jeremy whispered and turned toward them. "We'll do it."

"Great!" Eddie said and sighed. "Now, what do we do about Vexy?"

"Vexy? Oh… that's right," Matthew said and walked over to her room. "We should bring her along with us."

"Why?" Jeremy asked him. "We don't even know if we can trust her or not."

"Of course we can!" Matthew told him. "You saw her run out of the forest! She was terrified!"

"It could have been an act," Jeremy pointed out.

"It wasn't an act," Matthew argued and opened the door.

He entered the room and caught sight of Vexy, staring out the window. Slowly, she turned around to face him. Matthew immediately stopped walking when he noticed the tears streaming down her face.

"You're thinking about tossing me back out there, aren't you, Your Highness?" she asked him, wiping her tears away.

"No," Matthew answered and chuckled at the fact that she assumed he was Jeremy.

"It's okay. Your friends are wise to not trust me," she said and sniffled. "After all, I am the enemy."

"I don't feel that way," he assured her, taking a step closer.

"I was taken from my home... and *forced* to join Shane's army," she explained. "I never agreed."

"We know that. You're going to come with us," he said and reached his hand out for her. "Come on. It'll be fine."

Vexy placed her hand in his and smiled at him. He brushed the hair out of her face and returned the smile.

"Thank you," she whispered.

He merely nodded and opened the door for her. "By the way... I am Matthew," he said and smiled.

"Oh," she said and chuckled softly. "I'm sorry."

"It's okay," he replied and followed her into the hallway. "It's all part of our plan."

"Plan?" she asked and looked at Sheila.

Sheila was dressed in one of Jade's shiny green gowns with a silver robe and hood covering her head. Underneath her gown; however, was a pillow, to portray a very pregnant Jade.

"Wow, you look great, Sheila!" Matthew said, approaching her.

"Thanks," Sheila said and chuckled. "I feel silly."

"You see?" Matthew said and looked at Eddie. "I'm not the only one!"

Jade then walked out of the room she and Sheila had been in and stood at Jeremy's side, watching out the window.

"I do not feel right about this," she whispered to him.

"I know," he replied quietly. "But it's a good plan."

"I do not want to see hundreds of Pixadairies parish... because of me," she said and held onto his hand.

"I don't either," he said and turned to her. "But we have to protect our baby."

"Yes. I know," she whispered and looked down.

"Sir?" Reet's voice appeared out of nowhere. "I am here... what is going on?" he asked, out of breath.

"Reet! Wonderful!" Eddie said and walked toward his voice. "We need you to fly us out of here."

Reet was silent.

"Reet? Are you there?" Eddie asked, looking around.

"I am here," Reet replied, his voice low.

"Well... we need you to fly us out of here," Eddie repeated.

"I- I can't," he replied and scoffed. "I can't leave now."

"Reet, please," Matthew said, and walked over to stand by Eddie. "This is our chance to lead the Cembalotes away from Jade and your people."

"No," he said. "My children are here. I am not leaving them behind."

"Reet," Jade said softly and stood in front of the location of his voice. "Your children will be fine."

"How do you know? Are you going to go out there and keep them with you?" he asked her.

"Wait," Jeremy interrupted. "Reet, where *are* your children?"

"Risa is home with the tutor, and Kibtelo is with a group of friends," he answered and sighed. "I didn't even get a chance to get them to safety."

"Well, if Eddie's plan works, your children will be safe from harm," Jeremy told him.

"Okay," Reet agreed. "As long as this plan works... and my children remain safe."

"If anything goes wrong, Reet, I promise that I will find them... and bring them to the bunker," Jeremy said softly and smiled. "I promise."

"Okay, guys... we need to get moving," Eddie suggested.

"Right. Vexy goes with us, and Amber stays with you," Matthew said and grabbed Vexy's hand.

"You sure about that?" Jeremy asked him.

"Never been more sure about anything," he answered and looked at Vexy.

"Okay, then," Eddie said and looked at Jeremy and Jade. "You guys be safe... and take good care of Amber."

Jade looked down at the little girl and said, "Always."

"You guys be safe," Jeremy said and hugged Eddie tightly.

"We will," Eddie replied.

Jeremy released his grip on Eddie and looked over at Matthew. "Matt," he started and approached him. "I am so proud of you for this."

Matthew looked down and smiled softly. "I am more proud of you… for everything," he told him and hugged him. "I love you, brother."

"I love you, too," Jeremy whispered.

Matthew and Jeremy let go of one another. Jeremy grabbed Jade's hand tightly, while Matthew took hold of Vexy's.

Jeremy, Jade, Amber, and Boone stood in the hallway and watched as Eddie, Sheila, Matthew, and Vexy departed.

"I sure hope they know what they're doing," Jeremy said and sighed.

"The plan will work, Jeremy," Jade assured him. "It has to."

FIVE

Sua Deg

"We're approaching!" Reet shouted from the front of the aircraft.

Matthew and Vexy walked toward the front of the aircraft and looked out the window at the beautiful world ahead of them.

"This is Sua Deg?" Matthew asked, leaning on the back of Eddie's chair.

"Sure is," Reet replied. "Sua Deg... land of wizardry and magic."

"Umm... listen, guys," Vexy said, nervously. "When we land, I am going to stay here, ok?"

Matthew immediately turned to her. "What? No! You can't."

"Why can't I?" she asked him.

"Have you forgotten the army of Cembalotes trailing us?" he pointed out. "If you stay here, they'll find you."

Vexy chuckled nervously and shook her head. "Pardon me," she said quietly. "My mistake."

"Well, why did you want to stay here?" Sheila asked her.

"Nothing, nevermind," she said and walked toward the back of the plane.

Matthew, Sheila, Eddie, and Reet remained at the front of the ship. They looked out the window as they grew closer to Sua Deg. The bright blue sky sparkled with streams of purple light as they cut through the atmosphere.

"Are the Cembalotes still behind?" Eddie asked, attempting to look behind him.

"Yes," Reet replied as the monitor for the rear camera self-adjusted.

"Good," he said and sat back in the chair.

As Reet landed the airship, Eddie, Matthew, and Sheila continue to investigate this magical world in complete awe. The ground appeared to be covered in blankets of bright blue flowers and plant life. The buildings across the way stood tall and decorated with multi-colored glistening stones and gems.

"I have never seen anything like this in my life," Sheila said quietly, removing the hood from her head.

"Me neither," Matthew said and chuckled in joy.

"You haven't seen anything yet," Reet informed them.

As the aircraft landed, Reet released the handle to open the side hatch, allowing the teenagers to disembark. Eddie stepped down first, placing his feet down onto the mushy blue ground.

"Wow, this feels funny," he said and laughed.

Matthew exited second, also amazed at the feeling under his feet. Sheila placed the hood upon her head and walked down the ramp and onto the ground.

"The ground is saturated with remnants of used magic," Reet explained.

The teenagers watched as a handful of blue dirt hovered in the air from Reet's hand. He then sprinkled the dirt on the ground, causing dozens of flowers to bloom instantly.

"See?" he asked them.

"That's amazing," Sheila said and attempted the trick herself.

"Reet, how come you know so much about this place?" Matthew asked him.

"Long story, Matthew," he answered and sighed.

"Hey, guys," Eddie spoke up. "Where's Vexy?"

Instantly, the three teenagers turned their attention to the ramp of the airship. Matthew walked over and took a step onto the ramp.

"I'm here," Vexy said quietly, emerging from inside the airship.

"Good, we thought we'd lost you," Matthew chuckled.

"Not quite yet," she said and smiled nervously.

Just then, the teenagers caught sight of the airship containing the Cembalotes landing a few hundred feet away.

"Come on!" Reet shouted.

"Where can we go?" Eddie asked him.

"I know a place," Reet told him.

The teenagers and Vexy ran, following the sounds of Reet's footsteps. He led them through the fields and toward a small cottage built from tree branches and leaves that appeared to be purple.

"What's up with the purple leaves?" Matthew asked as he stopped running. He pointed to the cottage. "Over there," he said and pointed out in front of himself.

"Yeah, if the ground is blue from left-over magic... then what is purple?" Eddie added.

"Purple is magic that is currently in use," Reet answered and sighed. "We ought not to bother the creature that lives there."

Slowly, he began to walk in the direction leading away from the cottage. Almost immediately; however, he was interrupted by an arrow flying fast through the air toward him. The teenagers heard the sound of a body falling to the ground.

"Reet?!" Sheila called out.

"I'm alright," Reet said, his voice trembling.

"What was that?" Eddie asked, approaching Reet's voice.

"Someone shot an arrow in this direction," Reet replied.

The teenagers watched as an arrow seemed to extract itself from a nearby tree and slowly levitate toward them.

"See?" Reet asked as he held the arrow up for them to see.

Instantly, the teenagers looked around in hopes of visualizing their attacker. Matthew gasped and pointed to his right. The others immediately looked in that direction and caught sight of a creature approaching them at a distance.

"Is it a Cembalote?" Eddie asked.

"No," Reet replied as he dropped the arrow to the ground. "It's a Ladaquitte."

Matthew scoffed and asked, "what the hell is a Ladaquitte?"

Before Reet was able to answer that question, the creature appeared to grow wings that spanned ten feet across. The teenagers stood in awe as they watched the creature take flight and hover above them, gazing down.

"What is it doing?" Matthew asked, conjuring up his power timidly.

"Not sure," Reet answered.

Just then, the creature lowered itself to the ground, landing directly in front of Vexy. Stunned, she remained still, gazing at the creature's magnificent wings.

"Vexy… Get over here," Matthew whispered and reached for her.

The creature immediately reached over and pulled Matthew's hand away, hissing loudly. The teenagers continued to stare at the strange creature, which appeared to be human in shape and form. The teenagers could not determine anything about this creature, because of the dark brown cloak it wore, covering its entire face. Its hands and arms were identical to that of humans, but it possessed an impressive set of shimmering gold wings.

"Excuse me?" Eddie addressed the creature, taking a step toward it.

"Eddie, don't do that," Reet warned him.

"Reet?" the creature asked in a raspy feminine tone, turning its head in the direction of his voice. "Reet Calhausen?"

"Yeah," he answered, perplexed at the creature's acknowledgment of him.

The creature chuckled slightly and proceeded to relax its wings. The teenagers watched as the magnificent gold wings folded behind the creature's back and disappeared. Then, the creature took a step back and pulled the hood from its head.

Amazed, the teenagers gazed into the face of a horribly grotesque elderly female creature. Her face was covered with warts and wrinkles. It almost appeared as if the creature wore a rubber mask. She appeared human-like, but was obviously not of the same species.

"Who are you," Reet asked her.

"I am Mariette Bel Vista," she answered. "I am the first line of defense on Sua Deg."

"Great, so how do you know me?" Reet asked her, remaining puzzled by her.

"Nevermind that," she said and aimed her bow and arrow at Vexy.

"Wait! What are you doing?!" Matthew yelled, pushing Vexy out of the way.

Mariette released the arrow a second after Matthew pushed Vexy to the ground, saving her life. Frustrated, Mariette raised her bow once more, aiming at the Cembalote.

"Stop it!" Matthew screamed, standing up to face Mariette. "Someone stop her! Reet!" he screamed.

Instantly, Eddie plunged into Mariette, throwing her to the ground. The creature stood to her feet and began to expand her wings once more.

"Mariette!" Reet called out. "We mean you no harm."

"The Cemablote must be destroyed," Mariette warned them, pointing to Vexy. "Do not interfere, or you all will be destroyed as well!"

"Wait! Now, calm down!" Reet called out to her as she began to flap her wings. "We just need some help... please... please just help us, Mariette."

Mariette ceased to flap her wings and looked down at the frightened teenagers. Then, she turned her attention to Vexy.

"I will not help you while you are in the company of a Cembalote," she announced to them.

"But, she's not like the rest of them!" Matthew explained. "She's a good Cembalote!"

"There is no such thing," Mariette argued. She then turned and began to walk toward her cottage. "Get rid of her, and then we'll talk."

The others remained standing still, watching her every move. When Mariette realized they were in the same position, she turned and motioned for them to follow her.

"Should we follow her? She seems a little crazy," Sheila whispered to her friends.

"The Ladaquitte species rely on the fact that they remain completely delusional… especially to outsiders," Reet explained. "But she's just doing her job."

"She just tried to murder Vexy!" Matthew protested.

"Cembalotes are not a favorite on Sua Deg," Reet told them. "Why do you think I led the others here?"

The teenagers looked at each other as the sounds of Reet's footsteps were heard leading away from them. Eddie looked at Vexy and shrugged his shoulders.

"Maybe it would be best if you stayed here," he suggested to her.

"Wait, no!" Matthew protested. "We're not going to leave her here!"

"Matthew, Mariette will not help us as long as Vexy is here," Eddie said and put his hand on Matthew's shoulder. "It's our only choice right now."

"I'll go back to the ship," Vexy said and turned to walk away. "It's okay."

"Well, then… I'll go with you," Matthew told her and approached her.

Vexy immediately stopped, and turned to him. "It's okay… I'll be fine."

"I'd feel better if I were with you," he said and smiled.

"Matthew, please. Go with your friends," she instructed. "I'll be there when

you get back."

"That really is the safest place for her, Matthew," Sheila added. "If Mariette *is* the first line of defense on Sua Deg, then Vexy will be safe at the airship."

Matthew took a deep breath and said to Vexy, "alright. We'll come back to get you."

Vexy nodded her head and walked in the direction of the airship. Eddie, Matthew, and Sheila turned around and walked toward Mariette's cottage.

Vexy's breathing increased as she made her way through the fields leading to the airship. She then caught sight of a small group of Cembalotes investigating the area around her airship. Quickly, she ducked down to the ground in order to avoid detection. To her own dismay; however, her attempt to remain hidden was discovered.

"Sir!" a young male Cembalote called out, pointing in Vexy's direction.

Vexy remained on the ground, breathing hard while she heard the sounds of footsteps approaching. Panicking, she pulled her head down into the ground and covered it with her arms.

"Up!" Timothy ordered, kicking Vexy lightly in the side. He stood above her with his weapon aiming directly into the back of her head.

Instantly, she pulled her hands away from her head and held them out to show that she was unarmed. Keeping her head down and out of sight, she stood to her feet.

"Now, who are you?" Timothy asked her, pulling her head up to face him.

As Timothy looked into her face, he immediately gasped and dropped his weapon. As did the additional Cembalote soldiers standing at his side. Vexy chuckled and shook her head.

"What are you doing here, Timothy?" she asked him.

"Velexia," Timothy spoke as his jaw remained open from the sudden shock.

"Go on back," Vexy instructed, grabbing his weapon from the ground.

"Vexy, what are you doing here?" Timothy asked, taking the weapon from her hand.

"Mason, how are you?" Vexy asked the Cembalote soldier standing beside Timothy. She then turned and walked toward the Cembalote airship, ignoring Timothy's question.

"Vexy, wait!" Timothy called out, running after her.

"What, Timothy?" she asked in frustration, turning toward him.

"I don't like the fact that you are here… on Sua Deg," he whispered.

"Listen, little brother… I do not like that fact that *you* are on Sua Deg," she said and grabbed him by the arm. "Now, you will collect your soldiers and get back to Artobealu."

"Vexy, I can't," he said and shook his head. "I have orders to follow those kids."

"You tell Shane that I have everything covered, okay?" she said and smiled. "Now, get going before you are discovered… I wouldn't be able to live with myself if something happened to you."

"But, what are you doing here? And with those kids… why are you with them?" he asked as she pushed him up the ramp to his airship.

"Don't worry about it, Timothy. I've got it covered from here," she said and proceeded to push the remaining Cembalote soldiers toward the ramp. "Now, please. Go back where you're safe."

The front door opened, and Eddie entered the cottage first. Matthew followed him, with Sheila entering last. Mariette stood in front of a fireplace and turned toward the teenagers.

"That was a wise decision," she told them.

"What was?" Eddie asked her.

"Losing the Cembalote," she answered.

"Yeah," Matthew grumbled and sat down in a chair next to the door. "I don't see why it was necessary."

"Do you want my help… or not?" Mariette asked, approaching him.

"What's the big deal?" Matthew protested. "Reet brought us here so the Cembalotes would follow us… which, by the way, they did. So what if we were in the company of one?"

"You still do not understand," Mariette said and shook her head. "Cembalotes are not welcome on Sua Deg. It doesn't matter if it is one… or one hundred."

"Matthew, I think it's best if we honor Mariette's wishes," Reet suggested.

"Alright," Matthew agreed. "But, first… tell me what the big deal is about Mariette."

"She's a Ladaquitte," Reet answered him. "That should be a sufficient enough answer."

Matthew scoffed and rolled his eyes. He crossed his arms and leaned back in the chair, looking away from the others. Eddie and Sheila turned their attention away from their pouting friend, and gazed at Mariette.

"What is it that you need my help with?" Mariette asked them.

"Well... geez... I don't even know where to begin," Eddie answered and laughed. He placed his hands to his forehead and sighed deeply.

"Our friends on Artobealu have a very powerful stone, and the Cembalotes arrived and waged a war to retrieve it," Sheila spoke out. "So, we tried to make it look like we had the stone so they'd follow us... leaving our friends alone."

"Were you successful?" Mariette asked.

"I think so, yeah," she answered. "They did follow us."

"Wait," Mariette suddenly spoke. "What stone do your friends have?"

"It's the Black Onyx," Sheila replied.

Mariette fell silent. Slowly, she turned away from them and put her head down. Upon seeing her reaction, Matthew ceased his sulking and looked over at her.

"Mariette? What is it?" Eddie asked her.

"How... how can your friends posses that stone?" she asked them, continuing to look away.

"Well, *I* had it, actually," Sheila answered.

"*You*?!" Mariette asked, immediately turning to face her. "How did *you* have it?"

"I have no idea," she replied.

"No... no, it can't be," Mariette argued, approaching her.

"Well, it's true," Matthew claimed, standing to his feet.

"This can't be," Mariette mumbled, pacing around the room in front of the teenagers.

"What's the problem, Mariette?" Reet asked her.

"That stone is very dangerous," she answered. "You must get it back, and destroy it immediately."

"How are you supposed to destroy a stone that invokes invincibility?" Matthew asked.

"We can," Mariette asked, pointing out the window. "We Ladaquittes can destroy it."

"Well, what if we don't want to destroy it?" Eddie asked. "Our friends need it."

"No, they do not need the evil that accompanies it," Mariette explained. "Death follows that stone... always."

"Umm… okay," Matthew scoffed and rolled his eyes. "From what we understand, the person with the stone cannot die."

"You're forgetting one thing," Mariette started. "People without the stone can."

SIX

Choice

Jeremy took a deep breath and sat down on the last cot in the bunker. He held his forehead in his hands and slowly shook his head. Jade took a seat next to him and placed her hand on his leg.

"Jeremy?" she asked quietly, looking at the side of his face.

"You do understand that I cannot fathom what you've just told me, right?" he asked, looking up at Amber.

The little girl stood facing him. She tilted her head to one side and crossed her arms. Her composure did not change, regardless of Jeremy's reaction.

"It's completely absurd!" he argued, throwing his hands up in the air.

"What I've told you is the absolute truth," she claimed. "It's not my fault you don't believe me."

"How can I?" he asked, standing to his feet. He walked toward her and looked down in her face. "There is no possible way that you are who you claim to be."

"Anything's possible," she argued, sitting down on a nearby cot.

"Not this," he said and turned his back to her.

"Jeremy," Jade said, standing up to face him. "It is true. Everything Amber has said… is true."

"I'm sorry, Jade... But, I don't buy it," he whispered, looking into her face.

"But, she is-," Jade started, but was interrupted by the sound of the door handle to the bunker turning.

"Get back!" Jeremy yelled at her in a whisper. He rushed over to Amber and threw her behind him.

Quickly, he ran to the door. He raised his right hand and began to invoke his power, aiming it at the door. At that moment; however, the door swung open violently, knocking Jeremy to the floor. Jade rushed to him, leaning down to his side. She then looked up to witness Shane walking through the entrance to the bunker. Following closely behind him, was his new recruit: a young Pixadairie. Jade immediately gasped when she realized who the young creature was.

"Kibtelo!" she yelled, standing to her feet.

Jeremy held his left arm up, holding her back, while he used his right hand to employ his power. He looked into his former friend's face in fury. Shane merely chuckled and pushed Kibtelo in front of him, using him as a shield against Jeremy.

"Kibtelo! What are you doing with him?!" Jeremy shouted, looking into the young Pixadairie's face.

"He said he could make me powerful," Kibtelo replied in a frightened voice.

"Kib... this is who killed your mother!" Jeremy explained, pointing his watery hand at Shane.

Kibtelo immediately looked up at Shane. Shane laughed and shrugged his shoulders.

"It was a long time ago," he justified. "I wasn't the well balanced individual that I am today."

In a quick moment, Shane pushed Kibtelo to the side and grabbed Jade by the arm. Jeremy immediately reached for her, but Shane created a blistering hot orb of flames in his hand and held it up to Jeremy's chin. He instantly backed away from Shane, staring nervously into Jade's frightened face.

"Don't try anything," Shane warned him, continuing to hold the flames in his hand. "I will light her up like the fourth of July."

"Okay, okay," Jeremy said quietly, raising his hands to show Shane that he would not use his power.

Shane held onto Jade tightly, keeping his eyes on Jeremy. Kibtelo stood at Jeremy's side, watching with tear-filled eyes, while Amber held onto Jeremy's leg, peering out from behind him.

"Wait," Shane said and chuckled. "What is Amber Drayke doing here?"

"Nevermind her," Jeremy answered sternly and pointed to Jade. "Please just leave Jade alone… please."

Shane laughed and looked down at Jade. "Well, Jeremy… I see you've been busy," he said, referring to Jade's delicate condition. "But don't think for one second that I will show mercy."

"Shane… what do you want?" Jeremy whispered.

"You know… what I want," he answered, holding onto Jade tighter.

"Do not do it, Jeremy," Jade spoke out.

"Shut up!" Shane yelled, squeezing Jade in his grasp.

Jade let out a painful gasp, which caused Jeremy to take a few quick steps toward them. Shane instantly looked up at him and expelled a ball of fire from his hand. Immediately, Jeremy raised his arm and pushed a strong stream of water from his palm, extinguishing the flames. He continued toward Shane, wearing an enraged expression on his face.

"Jeremy, I warn you to stop!" Shane yelled, placing his hand over Jade's abdomen. "You saw me pull the stone through Sheila! Imagine what kind of damage I can do here!"

Upon hearing those words, Jeremy instantly stopped in his tracks and looked into his adversary's face.

"Shane, I beg you," he spoke. "Please, don't."

"Then give me the stone," Shane ordered.

Jade shook her head to Jeremy. "Do not," she whispered.

"He'll kill our child if I don't," Jeremy told her.

"Think of all the other children that will die if you give him the stone," she pointed out.

"Well, he won't kill mine," Jeremy said and clinched his teeth in anger. "I'll give you the damn stone, Shane," he addressed him. "Then you let her go!"

"That's fair enough," Shane said and smiled.

Jeremy looked at Jade and nodded his head slowly. He then walked over to entrance to the bunker and sighed deeply. Jade struggled with Shane to become free of his grasp.

"Jeremy! Do not give him the Black Onyx!" she shouted.

Jeremy chose to ignore her. He exited the bunker and walked down the hall to the last door on the left. His hand shook as he struggled to enter the combination to the door lock. After he successfully completed the sequence, the door latch unhinged, creating three loud bangs which echoed down the dark hallway.

"Some time today!" Shane shouted at him from inside the bunker down the hall.

Jeremy wiped the sweat from his forehead and breathed heavily. He walked through the door to the room and looked ahead at a steel door at the back of the room. He placed the index finger of his right hand on a circular disc in the middle of the door and pressed hard. Instantly, the door lock released, and Jeremy stepped back.

Slowly, the door opened and Jeremy stepped through. In the middle of the room, stood a pillar five feet tall, with a single stream of light illuminating the clear glass case atop of the stone pillar. Jeremy approached the pillar and looked down at the glimmering dark stone sitting alone in its glass tomb.

He knew that removing the Black Onyx from its safe haven would ultimately result in death and destruction, but at this point he had no choice. Jeremy's mind filled with images of Shane and his reign on high with the Black Onyx clutched tightly in his grasp. He knew that nothing would stop Shane once he possessed the stone. But, he knew that Shane would destroy everything that he cared for, just to own the Black Onyx. Jeremy would not accept that. So, he quickly opened the glass case and grabbed the Black Onyx.

"Shane! I have it!" Jeremy shouted in the hallway as he approached the bunker.

Jeremy walked into the bunker and looked at Shane, with Jade continuing to struggle in his grasp.

"Give it here," Shane demanded, holding out his hand.

"No," Jeremy replied and held onto the Black Onyx tightly. "Release Jade first."

"Fine," Shane said and pushed Jade hard against the wall of the bunker.

She fell to the ground and held onto her abdomen as the apparent pain rushed through her body. Jeremy immediately ran to her side and placed his hand on her shoulder. He looked into her watery eyes and then up at Shane. Standing to his feet, he raised his palm and aimed directly at Shane.

"Jeremy, I am growing very tired of this routine," Shane said and sighed deeply. "Now, I let her go... along with your son, so give me the stone."

"Jeremy, no," Jade whispered up to him.

"Don't do it, Jeremy!" Amber shouted from the opposite end of the bunker.

"You stay out of it!" Shane yelled at her, turning in her direction.

Jeremy took advantage of Shane's distraction, and leveled him with a powerful amount of water from his hand. Falling to the ground, Shane yelled out in fury and blocked Jeremy's power by creating a shield with his forearms.

Jeremy continued to shoot water at him, nonetheless. With incredible rage, he used all of his energy to increase the pressure of water striking Shane. Jade stood to her feet and signaled to Kibtelo and Amber to run toward her. The frightened youngsters jogged in her direction, but were stopped by Shane.

He continued to hold his right forearm upward, blocking Jeremy's power, but removed his left to grab Kibtelo as he attempted to run past. Holding onto the young Pixadairie, Shane let out a devious laugh and placed his hand over Kibtelo's chest.

"Jeremy! He has Kibtelo!" Amber yelled out, holding onto Jade's arm.

Jeremy instantly ceased evoking his power and looked at Shane. Breathing heavily, he shook his head at his old friend.

"Don't," he said.

"It's too late," Shane warned. "You should have given me the stone when you knew everyone was safe."

"Shane," Jeremy pleaded.

Shane laughed and pushed against Kibtelo's chest, throwing a jolt of electricity through his body. The young Pixadairie immediately convulsed and fell to the ground.

"No!" Jade screamed, and took a step forward attempting to run to him. Jeremy reached his hand out to stop her, however.

Jeremy, Jade, and Amber watched as Kibtelo's body stopped shaking, and his eyes turned to black. Shane stood above his lifeless body and smirked. Breathing heavily, he reached his hand out to his three frightened adversaries.

"You could have avoided this," he said quietly. "His death is no one's fault but your own."

"You did not have to do that," Jade said, crying.

"Yes, I did," he whispered. "Now, give me the stone… and I will spare your lives."

Jade buried her face in Jeremy's chest and let out a shattering cry. Amber stood beside Jeremy's leg with her arms wrapped tightly around, and stared at Kibtelo, lying on the hard concrete floor of the bunker.

Jeremy sighed deeply and looked down at the most recent victim of the battle for the Black Onyx. He placed his right hand on Jade's back to comfort her. With his left hand; however, he held out the Black Onyx for Shane.

Without hesitation, Shane approached him and took the stone from his hand. Holding the dark stone in his hands, he felt a sense of remarkable power that he had never experienced before.

"Hey, thanks," Shane said to Jeremy and walked toward the door to the bunker. "Oh, and if you ever try to retrieve this stone from me… just think about him," he warned and pointed to the dead Pixadairie before them.

Jeremy lowered his head and held onto Jade tightly. Shane watched them for a moment and laughed to himself.

"See ya," he said and walked out of the bunker and into the dark hallway.

SEVEN

UNSTOPPABLE

As Shane exited the castle, his army of Cembalotes threw their arms into the air and cheered loudly for his accomplishment. The echoing sound of thousands upon thousands cheering was deafening to the ears, but well worth it. He reveled in his fame, and in his new role as untouchable... unstoppable.

He looked around at the sight of endless bodies that littered the ground. As he watched his army lead countless Pixadairian soldiers to a makeshift prison, a smile arose to his face. His newfound power swam through his veins like piranhas on the hunt, and it felt good. With the stone making itself home in his shirt pocket, he felt completely invincible.

He approached his army of Cembalotes and raised his hand to speak. Instantly, the cheering ceased and all eyes were on Shane.

"Today I have achieved a feat that was inevitable," he began. "Now that I have done so, I will need your services further. So, I will warn you just once. If you desert your post or your company... you will be destroyed! No questions. No answers."

The crowd of Cembalotes remained silent. They watched as Shane paced in front of them, looking for any signs of weakness or mutinous actions.

"This is the last job that you will ever have for the rest of your life!" he shouted. "And you will serve with pride… and with honor! But you will also serve for me, and only me!"

The army of Cembalotes let out an uproarious cheer and raised their weapons to the sky. Shane nodded his head and approached the Pixadairian prisoners. As he walked in front of the cage that they were being held in, he could hear the sounds of injured soldiers moaning and groaning.

"Let me tell you all something," he addressed them. "You now have the chance to be something better than you are… To be better than you were ever expected to be. But you only have this one chance."

"Whatever it is," a male Pixadairian soldier spoke out. "We're not interested."

"You're gonna wish you had been," Shane said and tilted his head to the side.

"We're not going to join you," the same soldier informed him.

"Very well," Shane said and sighed deeply. "But no one can say I didn't give you a chance."

The Pixadairian soldiers began to shout out in protest and push on the wire fence, attempting to free themselves. Shane laughed loudly and raised his hands in front of himself. Staring into the eyes of dozens of identical soldiers, he shook his head and proceeded to set them ablaze. His ears became immune to the cries and the screams of dozens of dying Pixadairies as they burned to death. Shane was suddenly interrupted; however, by a tap on his shoulder.

"Sir?" a Cembalote soldier spoke.

"Yes?" Shane asked, turning to him. Shane then looked at two Pixadairian soldiers under the Cembalote's control. "What is this?" Shane asked him.

"Sir, I found these two escaping to the towns," his Cembalote soldier answered.

"Is that so?" Shane asked and looked at the Pixadairian soldiers. "What are your names?" he addressed them.

"I am Colonel Hull Hexum," Hull answered in a shaky voice. "And this is Major Boone Ciero."

"A colonel *and* a major?" Shane asked excitedly. "Wow, I hit the jackpot."

"They were escaping to protect the townspeople," Shane's subordinate informed him.

"Well, they certainly do need protecting, don't they?" Shane asked and laughed. "Would you two be interested in doing a little dirty work?" he asked them.

"Joining you?" Hull asked him.

"Yeah, something like that," he answered.

"Depends," Hull said and looked at Boone. "Why did you leave the bunker?" he asked Boone.

"King Jeremy told me to," Boone answered quietly. "So I did."

Hull sighed deeply and looked at Shane. "What became of the king and queen?" he asked.

"Dead," Shane answered and smiled.

Hull closed his eyes and lowered his head. Boone did the same.

"So, are you in?" Shane asked them.

The two sullen Pixadairian soldiers nodded their heads slowly, never looking up at him.

"Okay," Shane said and sighed. "So, we're done with this God forsaken place," he said, walking away. "On to new horizons."

Eddie sighed deeply and asked, "how do you expect to destroy the Black Onyx?"

"You have been misled somehow," Mariette answered.

"What kind of answer is that?" Matthew asked her, standing to his feet.

"What do you know about the Ladaquitte species?" she asked them.

"Not a thing," Matthew replied.

"I think you must sit down," she instructed Matthew. "It is time for you all to know about my species. I feel that this information will be of use to you."

"Okay, let's have it," Matthew said, taking a seat.

"Ladaquittes are allotted a total of ten sessions with magic," she began, with the teenagers' undivided attention. "Three of which must be used before the age of twenty. One session must be used to determine an individual quality that a Ladaquitte will posses for life. My individual quality is obviously my wings and power of flight. Now, after we choose our individual power, we are forever held to this power. We can never change. So, then the two additional sessions are used to our liking. We do whatever we want. After the age of twenty; however, we are forbidden to use any magic to benefit ourselves. We must only use our magic to help others."

"That's awful," Matthew spoke out. "You have all this magic, but you can't use it for yourself."

"Yes. I have seven sessions left, but can only use them for others," she replied.

"Mariette, if I may interrupt," Reet spoke up. "We're a little pressed for time... so, if we may speed this up a bit?"

"Certainly," she agreed. "But do not take what I am saying lightly."

"I'm not, I promise you," he said.

"Okay," she said and nodded her head. "My father used three of his sessions for one very specific purpose," she continued. "To protect the daughters of his closest friend."

The teenagers immediately sat straight up in their chairs. "The Triads!" Eddie called out. "It was for the Triads, right? Your father was Maz!"

Mariette's face became blank. "You knew him?" she asked.

"Of him," Eddie answered. "Our friend- Matthew's twin brother is now married to Jade," he told her.

"Jade," Mariette whispered and smiled. "I haven't seen her in years."

"She's quite a bit different now," Sheila said and laughed. "Quite a bit."

"And Pearl and Ruby? How are they?" Mariette asked.

The teenagers became silent. Eddie and Sheila looked down at the ground, while Matthew cleared his throat.

"They were murdered," he answered her. "For stones that your dad said would protect them."

"Matthew!" Sheila shouted in a whisper.

"What? It's true! Her dad created worthless stones and handed them over to some very trusting souls," he said and rolled his eyes. "And they were killed for it."

"But," Mariette began, confused. "Those stones are *not* worthless," she told them.

"Uh, yeah they are," Matthew argued.

"You know this for a fact?" Mariette asked.

"Well, a former friend of ours- who just so happens to have infinite powers- told Jade that they are worthless," Matthew answered.

"Infinite?" Mariette asked and stood to her feet. "Where is he?"

"Well, the last time we checked he was on Artobealu," Matthew said. "Where our friends are."

"We must go," she instructed them. "We must hunt him down for what he has done."

"Now, wait a minute!" Matthew shouted and stood up as well. "You need to finish your story before we go anywhere with you."

"Very well," she said and exhaled. "The stones that my father created for King Aboul and his daughters are not worthless... *together*. They are worthless alone."

"What?" Eddie whispered as his mind scrambled around the thought of it.

"The diamond, garnet, and emerald must be placed together to be effective," she explained. "As long as the sisters remained together... they were safe."

"Oh, no," Sheila said and lowered her head. "Jade wasn't with Pearl and Ruby when... when they were killed."

"That's right," Eddie agreed. "Pearl and Ruby were... in the room... and Jade was- wasn't. The Cajhorians wanted to keep Jade alive... for Shane."

"So, are you saying that the Triad's stones have the same effect... as the Black Onyx?" Matthew asked Mariette.

"Even more so," she answered. "The Triadal stones can destroy the Black Onyx, along with the magic from a Ladaquitte."

"Did a Ladaquitte create the Black Onyx?" Eddie asked.

"No, that stone did not come from Sua Deg, or any Ladaquitte. We would never create something so evil," she replied.

"Then how did Aboul get his hands on it... and give it to his 'secret daughter'- Sheila?" Matthew asked.

"Sheila?" she asked and looked directly at her. "*You're* Sapphire?"

"No, I'm Sheila," she answered and scoffed. "I've been through this before; I wanna be a kid for a while, okay?"

"It's a great honor to meet you," Mariette said and bowed her head.

"Stop it," Sheila said. "I'm just a high school junior, okay? I'm not a Triad."

"Not yet," Mariette said and smiled. "But there will come a day when you will decide without a reasonable doubt that you will accept your destiny… and become what you were always meant to be."

"That may be… but that's a long way away," Sheila said and shook her head.

"So, what do we do now?" Eddie asked, rising to his feet.

"You must find the Triadal stones," Mariette answered. "It is the only way to defeat the Black Onyx. And, along with me, we can put an end to it, finally."

"The diamond and garnet… Oh! The only place that I can think of that they would be… is Universe Six," Eddie said, pacing across the room.

"And the emerald is on Artobealu," Sheila said quietly.

"We should start with Universe Six," Reet suggested. "Get the hardest part out of the way."

"I agree," Mariette said. "That should be it, then."

"Alright, off we go," Eddie said and opened the door to Mariette's cottage.

"Wait," Mariette spoke up. "You must first know something," she informed them.

The teenagers stopped and turned to face her. She stood before them and inhaled deeply. With a slow movement of her hand across her face, the teenagers were amazed to witness her appearance alter dramatically. The elderly, wrinkled skin on her face transformed into a younger, smoother appearance. The warts that studded her face previously, became non-existent. Her hair was long and flowing, and gold in color. The torn brown robe she had been wearing fell to the ground to reveal a shimmering bright pink gown underneath. The teenagers stood in surprise as they looked into the face of a beautiful creature, much different than the creature they had been introduced to as Mariette Bel Vista.

"Wow," Matthew commented.

"Wh- why the disguise?" Eddie asked her.

"Ugly seems to turn everyone away," she answered. "Beauty causes curiosity. And curiosity is something Ladaquittes cannot afford to welcome."

"That makes sense," Matthew agreed. "I can completely understand that."

"Okay, now that we see the real you, Mariette… it's nice to meet you," Eddie said.

"And you as well," she replied and smiled.

The teenagers followed Mariette out of the cottage and through the wooded area in the direction of their airship. Sheila walked alongside Mariette, while Matthew and Eddie followed behind.

"Hey," Matthew said quietly to Eddie. He reached his hand out to stop Eddie from walking forward. "I gotta talk to you," he told him.

"What is it?" Eddie asked as he stopped walking to face his friend.

"I was wondering," Matthew began and looked down at the ground. "I was wondering if you were ever planning on telling Sheila how you feel about her."

Eddie chuckled and looked up at the sky. "Where did *that* come from?" he asked him.

"Everyone knows it… but her," Matthew replied. "I think before we proceed with this mission… you should tell her."

"What made you think of that? Why? Why would I possibly tell her now?"

"I- I just think you should," Matthew answered. "I think it's about time."

"Matthew, you're nuts," Eddie said and laughed. "I am *not* going to tell her now."

"If you don't… I will," Reet spoke up.

"What, do you eavesdrop now?" Eddie asked him and laughed.

"I'm sorry… I overheard, and I agree with Matthew," Reet told him. "I don't even know you all that well, but I can see how much you care for her."

"That's crazy," Eddie said and placed his hands on his head. "I haven't even made it obvious!"

"You didn't have to make it obvious for others to see it," Reet said and snickered.

Eddie then felt Reet's hand pat him on the side of his shoulder. "Thanks a lot, Reet," Eddie said, smiling.

"You gotta do it sometime, man," Matthew said.

"Alright," Eddie said and rolled his eyes. "I'll do it."

"Great!" Matthew said and turned to walk on. "You won't regret it!" he shouted as he walked away from Eddie and toward the airship.

Eddie folded his arms and shook his head as he watched his friends walk ahead. A blushing smile rose to his face when he began to imagine how he would feel when he would finally express his adoration for Sheila. He fantasized about her taking him in her arms and accepting his request to be together forever. He had always cared for her, but had never had the courage to let her in on the secret that his friends had known from the beginning.

As he approached the airship, he rehearsed what he would say to Sheila when he faced her. "I've always loved you," he whispered to himself, shaking his head at the sound of fear behind his voice. "You are the only person I have ever loved," he rehearsed again.

"Eddie!" Sheila suddenly shouted from inside the airship.

Her unexpected shrieking caused him to stop walking and immediately look up at the airship. "What is it?" he asked.

"It's Vexy!" she yelled. "Come quick!"

He instantly ran to the airship and darted up the ramp. When he approached Vexy, he looked into her fear-stricken face as she sat in a chair at the back of the airship.

"What's wrong?" he asked, kneeling down to face her.

"The Cembalotes were here," Matthew answered him for her. "They threatened Vexy, and almost killed her."

"Almost?" Eddie asked.

"Yeah, almost… but her brother is Shane's second-in-command, and he spared her life," Matthew informed him.

"Your brother? Your brother is fighting for Shane?" Eddie asked her.

"Yes, but not by choice," she answered quietly, staring straight ahead.

"Okay… Where did they go?" he asked her.

"They left," she replied. "They know that Cembalotes are killed if they land on Sua Deg, so they left."

"Was it the entire Cembalote army… or just a few?" Eddie asked.

"All," she answered. "Except for Shane."

"Too bad," Mariette commented and walked to the front of the airship.

"Great… that means that Jeremy, Jade, and Amber are safe, and our plan worked," Eddie said and sighed with relief. "Well, look… you're safe now," he told Vexy. "They're gone… and you're with us."

"I know," she whispered. "But I was so scared."

"It's okay," Matthew said and put his arm around Vexy.

Eddie and Sheila looked at one another. Eddie then smiled at her and held out his hand for her. "Come on, let's go to the front," he invited.

"Okay," she said and took his hand.

Reet ignited the engines to the airship and prepared to leave Sua Deg. Eddie and Sheila stood behind the captain's chair, while Mariette sat down in the co-pilot's seat.

"Are you ready for this?" she asked them.

"Absolutely," Eddie answered.

"Be sure," Mariette warned them. "This is not going to be easy."

Eddie looked over at Sheila and clinched her hand tighter. "I am sure," he said quietly.

Sheila looked up at him and returned the smile. "As am I."

Matthew sat with Vexy at the rear of the airship, holding onto her in attempt to comfort her. She rested her head on his shoulder and held onto his hand tightly.

"I'm sorry that we made you leave back there," he said to her quietly.

"It's okay," she replied. "I understand why."

"Mariette just has a serious problem with Cembalotes," he said and laughed softly.

"I'm not as bad as she thinks," Vexy explained. "I was just taken from my home and forced to join the army. I had no idea what we were about to do… or why."

"I believe you," he spoke.

"I had my own store, you know," she said suddenly and raised her head to look at him. "It was my own. I was proud of that."

"You owned a store?" he asked, perplexed.

"Yeah, a food store on Universe One," she answered.

Matthew immediately stopped breathing and looked into her face. "You lived on Universe One?"

"Well, yeah," she said and laughed. "Why is that such a shock?"

"But… don't criminals live there?" he asked, taking his hand away from her.

"Not all residents are criminals," she answered and sighed. "Have you been there before?"

"Yes! We were… and Eddie and I were drugged by your food," he scoffed and stood to his feet.

"Matthew, I assure you… we do not drug our food," Vexy validated. "I don't know where you got that from, but it's false."

"No, we lived it, okay? My friends said that we were not acting like ourselves, and Reet told us about how you drug your food to draw tourists in."

"Well, I didn't drug my food," she said and stood to face him. "But… I had something that no one else had."

"Which was?"

"In the cellar underneath my store… was a magical door that could lead you anywhere you wanted to go," she explained. "I discovered it by accident directly after I purchased the store."

"No one knew it was there?"

"Apparently not. Otherwise I would not have been able to buy the store… and everyone would've wanted to use the magic door."

"That must've been incredible," he commented. "Did you ever use it?"

"Yes," she answered. "I used to visit my family."

Vexy then looked down at the floor of the airship and sighed deeply. Matthew took notice to her sudden change in demeanor, and raised her chin so that she would look at him.

"What is it?" he asked her.

"It's just that... I hadn't seen my brother is such a long time. Then, he appears on Sua Deg under Shane's command. I didn't want my brother to be forced to fight as I was," she said and sobbed.

"Oh, don't cry," he said, pulling her closer to him. He wrapped his arms around her and said, "this will all be over soon, don't worry."

Vexy held onto Matthew and opened her eyes. Without letting him take notice, an evil smirk appeared on her face as she realized that her own deception had been successful. Matthew trusted her, as well as Eddie, Sheila, and Reet. This fact would ultimately be the cause of their downfall.

EIGHT

TRANSFORMATION

"Sir?" Mason asked, approaching Timothy.

Timothy turned around from behind the pilot's chair and nodded to his subordinate. "What is it, Mason?"

"I really do not want to be a part in hurting those kids," he replied quietly.

"To tell you the truth," Timothy began and sighed. "I don't either. But, we have orders. And now, we're supposed to turn around and follow those kids... and capture them."

"But, you're second-in-command," Mason pointed out. "You can order us to abort this mission and go home."

"No, I can't, Mason. You know that I cannot do that," Timothy reminded him. "I have gotten word that Shane has retrieved the Black Onyx. You know what that means? That means there is no stopping him now. So, we are stuck and obligated to serve him... indefinitely."

"But your sister is in cahoots with him," Mason whispered. "Maybe you can talk to her about getting us out."

"Have you not realized yet that Vexy is just as evil as Shane?" Timothy asked him and threw his arms up in frustration. "She'll have us destroyed for mutiny!"

"She wouldn't destroy *you*."

Timothy paused at Mason's words and looked straight into his gray eyes. "She would make an example out of me," he spoke sternly. "I would be the first to go."

Jeremy placed his hands over his tear-filled eyes and knelt down to Kibtelo's body. He sat and sobbed as Jade and Amber held onto each other, weeping quietly.

"It's all my fault!" Jeremy sobbed. "I should have given Shane the stone."

"Jeremy," Jade whispered and knelt down next to him. "This is not your fault."

"Yes, it is," he said and looked at her.

She gently wiped the tears from his cheeks and held onto his hand. "You did what you had to… in that moment," she spoke. "No one blames you."

"How can I face Reet now?" he asked. "I promised him that I would keep his children safe."

"There was so much going on, Jeremy. You could not have known that Shane found Kibtelo," she told him. "I will speak with Reet when he returns."

"No," Jeremy said and wiped his eyes. "I am not going to have you do something that shouldn't be your place to do. This was my doing. So, I will deal with the consequences."

"Jeremy," Amber spoke out and knelt to his side. "Do not blame yourself for what has happened here today. Kibtelo's death was a result of the Black Onyx, and the evil it emits."

"Well, with that being said… I am going to find Risa Calhausen and keep her safe no matter what," Jeremy said and stood to his feet.

He walked away from them and toward the door to the bunker. Jade and Amber stood up as well and followed him into the dark hallway.

As they opened the castle door and walked outside, Jade instantly gasped and fell to her knees. Jeremy and Amber ran to her and helped her to stand up.

"What has happened?!" she shouted as she looked around at the death and destruction left behind from the Cembalotes.

"Are they gone?" Amber asked, looking around as well.

"Yeah," Jeremy answered quietly and walked ahead to the makeshift prison in front of the castle.

He stood in front of the metal wire that had kept the prisoners locked up, and lowered his head at the sight. The charred bodies of unarmed Pixadairies lay on the ground. The smoke from the deadly fire continued to rise from the lifeless bodies. Jeremy exhaled deeply and placed his hands on the fence, lowering his head to look at the ground.

Jade approached him and placed her hand on his back. "What has he done?" she whispered. "Those poor creatures."

"I'm going to get him for this," Jeremy said in a quiet, enraged voice. "If it's the last thing I do."

"How?" Jade asked and chuckled slightly. "He is untouchable now. He has the only stone in existence with enough power to rule… everything and everyone."

"I'll do it, Jade," Jeremy professed. "Someway, somehow, someday, I will get him."

At that moment, sounds of numerous footsteps were heard from behind them. Jeremy immediately invoked his power and placed himself in front of Jade. He sighed deeply when he realized the footsteps were from several Pixadairian civilians. The water dissolved from his hand as he disabled his power.

Dozens of Pixadairians approached them, and stared helplessly at the bodies of their brave soldiers. Jade wiped her wet cheek and reached out her hand for one of the young Pixadairies. He walked over and held onto her in grief.

"My father didn't come back," he whispered to her in a sullen voice.

"I know," she said, stroking his back to comfort him.

Suddenly, Jeremy caught a glimpse of Reet's youngest child, and Kibtelo's sister. Immediately, he ran to her.

"Risa," he spoke and knelt down to face her.

The young female looked into her king's face and began to cry. He held onto her tightly and ran his hands through her dark hair. He then picked her up, carrying her as he walked back to join Jade and the others.

He stood in front of the frightened creatures, with Risa clinging to him in his arms. He then began to look out at the grief-filled faces of the identical creatures.

"I don't know where to begin!" he called out, addressing them. "We were defeated by an enemy that we didn't even know was there."

He continued to stroke Risa's hair as she sobbed. Jade then stepped in front of him and looked out at her people.

"Has anyone seen Colonel Hexum and Major Ciero?" she asked them.

"They joined the Cembalotes!" a male voice answered from the crowd.

"What?" Jade asked quietly and looked at Jeremy. "Why?"

"They were told you were dead!" the same voice spoke. "We were told the same!"

"Yeah! Where were you?!" an additional voice asked angrily.

"We couldn't… we had a plan to get rid of the Cembalotes," Jeremy explained. "Obviously, it didn't work."

"No kidding!" a third voice yelled. "What do we do now?!"

"Now? Now we wait for my friends to return," he answered. "We can't fight back alone."

"Fight back?" Jade asked, turning toward him. "No, you heard him; he will kill us if we go after that stone. I do not want to put our son in the position to be destroyed again… We have to keep him safe."

Jeremy paused and looked down into her face. He took a deep breath and nodded his head, agreeing with her. "I will not do anything until our baby is born," he whispered. "Then, after that… Shane had better watch his back."

Matthew took a seat next to Vexy in the rear of the aircraft. He looked down at his brother's clothes that he was wearing and sighed, shaking his head.

"What is it?" Vexy asked him.

"Jeremy," he replied. "He really is something else."

"What do you mean?"

"Just look at these clothes!" Matthew said and pointed to his shirt and pants. "Only he would wear something so ridiculous."

"Maybe it's not ridiculous to him," she pointed out. "Not everyone dresses like humans of Earth. Just look at me," she said and pointed to her white gown.

"Well, alright," Matthew said and laughed. "I guess you're right. I just miss him, you know? We used to be so close."

"You can still be close," she told him. "He just has a lot more responsibility now."

"Yeah, I know," he said and placed his hands on his forehead. "Did you know that Jeremy is a swimmer?" he asked, looking over at her.

"N-no, I didn't," she answered, confused by his sudden change of subject.

"Oh, yeah… he's good enough for the Olympics," he told her.

"What are the Olympics?" she asked.

"Oh, the Olympics are events in which people compete in similar sports; such as swimming," he answered her. "Well, Jeremy could have gone… and won."

"He's that good?"

"I'll put it to you this way," he began and turned toward her in his chair. "Every single day of the summer, you could always find Jeremy in our neighbor's pool," he said and looked down. "She was an old bat," he said and laughed. "She didn't like any of us neighborhood kids… but for some reason, she took to Jeremy. She always let him use her pool, no matter what. Of course, he would sneak us in when she wasn't home."

Vexy looked into Matthew's sincere face and smiled.

"Anyway," he said and looked at her. "The old bat would let us neighborhood kids hold a competition at the end of summer. You know, me, some other neighborhood kids, Jeremy, Eddie… and Shane," he told her and looked back down. "Yeah, even Shane."

"Unbelievable," Vexy said and took his hand.

"Yeah, well… everyone knew that Jeremy was the best. He could beat *anyone* in any swimming event," he said and smiled. "Obviously this year we didn't have an end-of-summer swim event, because we were stuck out here… But, last year's event will always be the most memorable."

"Why is that?"

"All of our parents showed up for it," he answered. "It was the first time since we started this event that our parents actually came up to watch. You see, we just held the event for fun… you know, just for us kids. Well, our parents decided that they wanted to make it more competitive.

"So, they each cheered for their own kid, and things changed within all of us. What I mean is, we weren't swimming for fun… we were swimming to win. To make matters even worse, our dad even showed up."

"Why is that bad?" Vexy asked him.

"Well, for about five years now, he's been in and out of our lives," he answered. "Call it business, call it personal… I don't really know which."

"I'm sorry to hear that," she said and looked into his blue eyes. "I'm sure that's hard on you and your brother."

"It's cool," he replied. "Jeremy and I found ways to deal with it… you know? He's got his swimming, and I've got my skiing."

"So, what happened at the swimming event?" she asked.

"Oh, right," he said and chuckled. "So, Jeremy had pretty much beaten everyone there… He was untouchable, and he reveled in this attention that he was receiving… especially from our dad.

"You know, Dad was standing on the side of the pool and screaming, 'get 'im, Jeremy! You can do it!' So, I think winning Dad's approval really made Jeremy push himself harder. I guess it would for anyone.

"Okay, so after Jeremy had beaten everyone, and was officially in first place, my father made a bet with Eddie's father. He bet him that Jeremy could beat me… in a race."

Vexy immediately looked at him. "Your father made a bet against *you*?"

"Oh, yeah… His argument was that Jeremy and I are twins, and should be equal… in everything, including swimming," Matthew answered. "But, he said that Jeremy was the better athlete. Of course, Eddie's father took that bet. He argued that Jeremy and I were both athletes, but excelled in very different sports. I think he wanted me to win… to show my father that I was just as good as Jeremy."

"Eddie's father defended you?" she asked.

"Yeah," he answered. "It's a shame that someone else's father knew more about me than my own did."

"So… what happened?" she asked, intrigued.

"Okay, so Eddie's father bet on me, while my own father bet on Jeremy," he started. "Oh, man... if you could have seen my father encouraging Jeremy to beat me by a mile... it was humiliating. I knew that Jeremy was enjoying being in the spotlight, so I had the mind-set to really give it my all in the race.

"I wanted to win my father's approval as well. Even though I excelled at skiing, my father had never seen me compete in an event. He was never around for them. But, he had seen Jeremy win dozens of races... You see, Jeremy was my father's pride and joy. He was the absolute favorite in our family."

"Why?"

"I never figured that one out," he answered. "So, instead of succeeding in my school work like Jeremy had, I made fun of the people that did," Matthew said and laughed. "If that makes any sense."

"You were jealous of him," Vexy pointed out.

"I had every reason," Matthew said and cleared his throat. "Anyway, Jeremy and I were set to race. He was on the left side of the pool, while I was on the right. The rules were simple: swim to the end of the pool, turn around and come back.

"Eddie and Shane stood on both sides of the pool and cheered for us equally... They knew that this race was bogus. It was just an attempt for my father to show Jeremy off to the neighbors once again.

"So, we were off. I knew right away that the race was over, because between breaths, I looked up and Jeremy was gone. But, I didn't give up. I kept kicking my feet, and pushing the water by me with my arms. I knew that beating Jeremy was never possible, but I didn't want to lose by quitting.

"As I made my way back on my second lap, I looked over and saw Jeremy; pacing himself to remain equal with me. I could hear my father's overbearing voice screaming at him to 'get the lead out'. But, he kept in time with me.

"I didn't understand it at the time, but when I finished the race, I heard an abundance of cheering from the people present. I looked over and watched Jeremy touch the side of the pool *after* I had. He popped his head out of the water and instantly smiled at me."

"He let you win?"

"Yeah, he did," Matthew replied. "Everyone was surprised... even me. After seeing that I had won, Eddie and Shane immediately cheered for me, and encouraged the shocked observers to do that same. It was at that moment that I knew that Jeremy would achieve greatness beyond everyone's imagination. Not only was he the best at pretty much everything, but he was also willing to sacrifice for others. Huh... I would say that Jeremy is my hero. He is the one person that I wish I could measure up to. It's funny... I am older than he is by fifteen minutes, but he is the bigger man."

"But, you're both so different in your own ways," Vexy validated. "I am sure that there are things about you that he wishes he could achieve."

"Thanks, Vexy," Matthew said and laughed. "But, I am sure you're wrong."

Just then, Eddie approached them from the front of the airship. "Matthew," he addressed him. "May I speak with you for a minute?"

"Sure," Matthew said and stood up. He walked toward Eddie and noticed the concerned demeanor upon his face. "What's up?" he asked him.

"Uh, well... we talked, and it probably would be best if you didn't offer too much information to Vexy," he replied in a whisper.

"Okay... and why's that?" Matthew asked.

"Mariette may be right," he answered. "We don't really know a whole lot about Cembalotes, Matthew."

"I think she's fine," Matthew scoffed and rolled his eyes. "I've been talking to her, and she hasn't even showed a *hint* of evil, Eddie. Jeez."

"Just don't tell her anything about where we're going, and what we're going to do," Eddie instructed and patted him on the shoulder.

"Fine," Matthew complied and returned to Vexy's side.

Eddie approached the front of the plane and sat down next to Sheila behind the co-pilot's chair.

"How'd it go?" she asked him.

"He's still stubborn as ever, but he agreed not to tell her anything," he replied.

"He has grown an admiration for her," Mariette commented, turning around to face him. "That's not a good thing."

"Well, I can't tell him who not to like," Eddie said and scoffed. "I felt awful just telling him to not disclose too much to her."

"You shouldn't," Mariette said. "She will show you her true side… eventually."

"Wait a minute," Sheila said and raised her hand to get Mariette's attention. "What do you have against Cembalotes, anyway? I noticed that when we mentioned to her that we were going to Sua Deg, she freaked out a little. She even said that she would stay on the ship. *And* you tried to kill her on sight. So, what gives?"

"Cembalotes are not welcome on Sua Deg," she answered.

"Yeah, I got that," Sheila said and nodded her head.

"A Cembalote tortured and murdered my father," she replied, looking straight into Sheila's face. "You got *that*?"

Sheila scoffed and shook her head. "Yes, Shane killed your father. But, that doesn't necessarily mean that all Cembalotes are evil."

"No, but from that point on, no Cembalote would ever be allowed to step foot on Sua Deg. Naturally, it took a few dead Cembalotes for the rest to get the idea," she explained. "We are not going to trust that species… ever again."

"So, you murdered innocent Cembalotes to prove your point?" Sheila asked her.

"Yes," she replied.

The teenagers became silent after Mariette disclosed that information. Then, Reet cleared his throat and asked her, "let me ask you this… upon first encountering us… how did you know *me*?"

"Every Ladaquitte knows about you and your unfortunate past," she answered. "We heard about the latest means for punishment originating from Artobealu. So, we have been trying to develop a way to reverse your invisibility."

"Wow," Eddie said and laughed. "It really is a small universe, huh?"

"What?" Mariette asked him, confused by his comment.

"Well, you've been trying to help Reet out… never actually knowing him… and here he appears on your world," he replied.

"I've been to Sua Deg before," Reet informed them.

Eddie then looked over to the pilot's chair. "When?" he asked him.

"Long ago," he said. "I actually met with Maz."

"You met with my father?" Mariette asked him.

"Yes… I suppose that is why you've heard of me," he told her. "When I was convicted of espionage and banished from my home, I traveled to Sua Deg to seek help. That is when I first met your father," he explained. "I was trying to find any way possible to fix what had been done to me… and I knew about your unique magic. Well, little did I know that Shane would ultimately kill him… because of information that I passed on to him… which got me in trouble in the first place."

"Oh, no… that's how Shane found out about Maz? From the documents that you had stolen?" Eddie asked him.

"Yes," he answered. "Everything from that point on was my fault; your father's death, the Triad's deaths, the war against universes, and eventually my own queen's death."

"Reet, you were just protecting your children," Sheila said, reaching her hand out to touch his shoulder.

"What good that did," he said quietly. "They're in a world that is probably under attack by now."

"No, remember what Vexy said?" Eddie pointed out. "The Cembalotes followed us to Sua Deg… remember? My plan worked."

"Not all of the Cembalotes," Reet said and sighed. "Remember? Vexy said that Shane had not come along. That means anything by this point."

"Do you want to continue going to Universe Six, or do you want to go back to Artobealu?" Eddie asked him.

Reet paused for a minute. Then, he answered, "no, we should go on to Universe Six. Jeremy gave me his word that he would keep my children safe, and I trust that he will keep it."

Shane held the Black Onyx in his hand and smiled at its reflective surface shimmering in the light of the lamp above his head. The shiny black stone was smooth to the touch, even around the edges.

"Sir, we're approaching," Hull informed him, walking into the back of the airship.

"Very good," Shane replied and tucked the stone back into his shirt pocket.

He stood to his feet and walked to the side of the airship. He glanced out the window and smiled when his discovered the perfect spot to build his new castle.

"Why did you choose Universe Four?" Hull asked, standing at Shane's side.

"It's simple, really," Shane answered, turning to face him. "There are only a few inhabitants to destroy, and claim this land as my own."

Hull swallowed hard as these words left Shane's mouth. "You're going to destroy them?" he asked.

"Of course," he replied. "From this point on, I will take no prisoners."

Shane then flashed him a crooked smile and walked away. Hull looked out the window as the aircraft landed. His heart raced as he clenched his hands in anger. He did not feel good about joining Shane's army, but felt that he had no choice. He did not want additional violence to fall upon Artobealu, so he felt that joining Shane would lead him away from his homeland.

Hull joined Boone by his side at the exit door of the airship and nodded his head. "It'll be okay," he said quietly.

"I don't feel right about this," Boone told him. "We shouldn't have left. We shouldn't have joined him... he killed Queen Jade and King Jeremy."

"We didn't have a choice, Boone," Hull told him. "He would have killed us, too... and those other kids are still out there. If we get the chance to help them, we will."

Boone nodded his head and walked down the ramp of the airship. He and Hull stood at the bottom and looked out at this new world. The land was perfectly flat, with red clay-like substance that made up the soil. Every so many feet, a single plant sprouted up through the soil, which appeared to be the only plant life in this universe. The atmosphere was thick and made it difficult to breathe at times. The only light that was provided on this universe was emitted from a small oval moon, which hovered high in the dark purple sky, giving off its silver color.

"Isn't it marvelous?" Shane shouted to his crew from a few hundred yards away.

The army of Cembalotes stood outside of the airship and watched their leader inspect his new territory. Hull and Boone remained at the bottom of the ramp, watching nervously.

Shane stopped looking around suddenly, and raised his right hand out in front of himself. The army of Cembalotes, along with Hull and Boone, watched as an unbelievable event began to happen.

From his hand, Shane began to build the foundation of what was to be his castle. Formed rock and gray stone appeared out of nowhere and situated on the ground in front of Shane. With a quick movement of his hand, he used his telekinetic power to move the rock and stone to his liking. After he built his foundation, he began work on the additional floors and roofing of the castle.

"Incredible," a member of the Cembalote army spoke quietly, as they watched the castle being constructed.

"I guess there really is nothing he can't do," another Cembalote commented.

"You have no idea," Hull said and shook his head.

Shane then turned around to face his army, out of breath. "Are you ready to see your new home?" he addressed them.

The army of Cembalotes reluctantly cheered for their leader. A few brave soldiers mumbled and grumbled underneath the sound of cheering from their peers. They were not happy to serve Shane, and wanted nothing more than to go home. But, out of fear for their lives, they had no choice but to comply with his demand.

"Then, let's go home," Shane said and turned to walk through the front door of the castle. "Shrink yourselves before entering!" he ordered.

Hull and Boone remained standing outside as members of the Cembalote army began to shrink themselves and enter the castle.

"Good luck to you both," a Cembalote soldier said to Hull and Boone.

They nodded to him and watched as he shrank himself down to the size of a thumb and walk toward the castle. Hull and Boone then looked up and gazed at the miraculous new structure before them.

The castle stood one hundred feet tall, with giant stained glass windows on every level. The stone that Shane had created to cover the outside of the castle was dark gray in color, with specs of silver throughout. The overly large door to the entrance opened like a drawbridge, and was operated only by Shane's thoughts. This structure was created with ingenious care, but from a demented mind.

Hull and Boone lowered their heads and entered the castle, paying close attention to the layout of the interior. The foyer was encased with impermeable steel with sharp, ten inch blades facing outwards.

"Watch yourselves," Shane spoke out.

Hull and Boone immediately looked up at him. As he closed his eyes, the drawbridge door slammed shut, and the foyer closed on itself, prohibiting escape, or exit.

"Dang, I'm good," Shane said and laughed, walking toward the nervous Pixadairies. "Now… about you two," he addressed them. "I realize that you both stick out like sore thumbs in my army."

"Sir?" Hull asked, looking over at Boone.

"Yeah! Your species is that of darker color… and my army is made up of light-skinned Cembalotes," he answered. "Anyone will be able to spot you from a mile away."

"Wh-what do you suppose we do about that?" Boone asked, nervously.

"Well, since you both come highly trained in combat situations, I reckon that I will leave you to your current ranks," he replied. "However… I cannot allow myself or my people to be seen sporting with Pixadairies. I just won't have it."

Hull and Boone took a step back, preparing themselves for what Shane was proposing.

"Now, don't worry yourselves," he said and laughed. "I'm not gonna kill you."

"That's good to know," Boone said and sighed.

"Nah, I'm not gonna kill you," Shane said quietly. "But… what I am going to do may sting a little."

"Sir?" Hull asked, taking an additional step backwards.

Shane did not speak. Instead, he took three steps toward the frightened soldiers. Slowly, he raised his hands until his arms were parallel to the ground. Hull and Boone instantly ran backward to the enclosed foyer. They pulled at the steel tomb, trying desperately to open it. Shane laughed and shook his head.

"You're gonna thank me for this," he spoke to them. "Trust me."

"Just, stop!" Hull pleaded. "Whatever you're thinking of doing… just stop!"

"Can't do it," Shane said and smiled.

Shane's hands were nearly touching the terrified soldiers, outstretched toward them. His body shook slightly as he gathered enough energy to perform the impossible. With his gray eyes glowing brightly, he pushed his power outwards through his hands and into Hull and Boone.

Instantly, they fell to the ground, writhing and groaning in pain. Shane stood above them, lowering his arms and struggling for breath, and watched their incredible transformation.

By this time, he was joined by several Cembalotes; who had remained two inches tall. They stood directly beside Shane's boot, and formed two straight lines across.

Hull and Boone continued to yell in agony as their skin began to lighten and clumps of their hair fell out to the floor. Shane reached out and held on to the wall in order to keep from falling over from lack of energy.

He watched with widened eyes as the Pixadairian soldiers' bald head began to sprout blonde hairs. Hull then looked up at Shane in incredible pain as his light blue eyes changed to gray.

Boone cried out as an additional transformation began to happen as well. He looked down in complete confusion as this happened.

Shane stood above him and chuckled as he realized what Boone was experiencing. "You'll thank me," he whispered down to him.

When their transformation was complete, they continued to lie on the cold, hard floor of the castle. Shane looked down at the gathering Cembalotes at his feet and scoffed.

"Alright," he spoke down to them. "You can return to normal now."

One by one, the army of Cembalotes reversed their shrinking ability, allowing themselves to be equal in height as Shane.

Hull then stood to his feet and looked into the faces of the stunned audience before him.

"What?" he asked, looking down at his hands in front of himself. "What did you do?!" he shouted at Shane.

"As I said before; I will not be seen with a couple of Pixadairies," he repeated. "So, now you're Cembalotes."

Hull gasped and looked down at Boone, who was struggling to his feet. "Boone, stand up!" he ordered.

"I'm trying!" Boone said painfully.

"Change us back!" Hull demanded to Shane.

"Nah," Shane said and laughed. "You look better this way." He then pulled a mirror off of the wall and held it up for them to see.

They immediately gasped at their appearance. Hull lifted his hand to his face and looked into his own eyes. Swallowing hard, he looked over at Boone, who wore a surprised expression on his face as well. They were no longer identical, which meant that they would have separate identities from that point on. Not only were they shocked by what they were seeing in the mirror, but they were angered by the fact that they looked like the species their soldiers had battled earlier that day.

"See? I knew you'd like it," Shane said and threw the mirror to the ground, breaking it into pieces. "I don't have bad luck," he whispered while looking down at the broken mirror, walking away from them.

He walked down the hall and entered the last room on the left. A weak beeping sound was heard through the room, coming from a communicator beside a large chair at the back of the room. Shane picked the receiver up and placed it to his ear.

"Sir?" Timothy's voice was heard through the receiver.

"Timothy," Shane started. "How's the tracking going?"

"We've located them, Sir," Timothy informed him. "It appears they're en route to Universe Six."

"Follow them, capture them, and inform me as soon as you do," Shane ordered. "But... keep them alive. If they are hurt in any way, I will hold you personally responsible."

"Sir, Vexy is with them," Timothy told him.

"Yes, Timothy... I know," Shane replied. "Per my orders."

"Um... What should we do about her?" he asked him.

"She knows what to do," Shane answered.

"Yes, Sir," Timothy said.

Shane set down the receiver and sighed. "What would they possibly want with Universe Six?" he asked himself.

He then sat down in the large chair and rested his head on the back support, placing his right hand over his eyes. Within an instant, he opened his glowing eyes and visualized his friends in that exact moment.

"What do we do if the Cajhorians want to battle?" Shane heard Eddie ask the others.

"We battle them," Mariette answered.

"I don't think I have the energy to face them again," Eddie said and sighed. "I felt like we just fought them."

"In reality," Sheila started. "We did."

"What if Sheila stops time right away," Matthew suggested, walking up toward the front of the ship, with Vexy at his side.

Shane clenched his fist as he watched Matthew grab Vexy's hand. He continued to witness the conversation, nonetheless.

"Yeah, that could work," Eddie said and turned to Sheila. "You up for it?" he asked her.

"Absolutely," she answered.

Shane shook his head. "What are you up to?" he asked himself, regarding his old friends. He then decided to use Vexy in a method to discover their intentions for going back to Universe Six.

"What are you planning to do?" Vexy asked them, letting go of Matthew's hand. As she asked this question, she looked down at her own hand in confusion as to why she had released it. Little did she know that Shane was using her as a puppet.

"Uh... we're going to recover some old items," Matthew answered nervously, turning to her.

"Oh, yeah?" she asked and looked up into his face, confused. "What items?"

"Nevermind that," Eddie said, standing up. "This is just something we've got to do on our own," he told her. "Right, Matthew?" he asked him.

"Yeah, he's right," Matthew said, looking down at Vexy. He then grabbed her hand once more, but she resisted. "What's the matter?" he asked her.

"Nothing at all," she answered as her eyes widened.

Matthew took notice to her strange behavior, and backed away from her slowly. "Vexy, what is it?" he asked.

"I'm fine, Matthew!" she answered, her eyes continuing to wander around the ship.

"You're not acting fine!" he told her. "It's like you're behind the wheel, but someone else is driving."

"No, not at all," she replied. "Everything's great!"

Shane chuckled to himself and decided to drop Vexy from his act. She instantly lowered her head and raised her hands to her ears. Matthew, Eddie, Sheila, and Mariette watched as she shook her head a few times and looked up at them.

"What is it?" Matthew asked her.

"I- I… nothing," she replied. "Sorry, I just get a little weird sometimes," she said, breathing heavily and wearing an expression of confusion and anger.

"That was like something out of 'The Exorcist'," Matthew commented and laughed. "Are you sure you're okay?"

"Yes," she answered and smiled weakly. "I'll just go in the back now." She then walked away from them slowly.

"What the hell was that all about?" Eddie whispered.

"I have no idea," Matthew said and chuckled quietly.

Shane shook his head, and his eyes returned to normal. He stood up from his chair and picked the receiver up once again. He pushed three buttons on the face of the communicator and waited for Timothy to respond.

"Sir?" Timothy spoke.

"Yeah, Timothy. There's something strange going on between Vexy and my old friend, Matthew," Shane informed him. "She didn't happen to mention anything to you, did she?"

"No, Sir," he answered. "Not a word."

"Alright. Well, you make damn well sure that you capture them before they do *anything* on Universe Six, got it?" he ordered.

"Of course, Sir," he complied.

"I'm counting on this, Timothy," Shane told him.

"You can count on us, Sir," he said.

"Oh, one last thing, Timothy," Shane said.

"Sir?"

"When you capture them… give Vexy the same treatment as the others."

Timothy paused for a moment. "Sir? You want me to capture my sister?" he asked him.

"Yes," he answered. "I want the others to believe that she is a victim as well."

"Very well, Sir," Timothy spoke.

NINE

Six Months In

Jeremy continued to hold Risa in his arms while he sifted through debris, searching for survivors of the attack. Jade assisted in returning missing youngsters to their parental units, while Amber helped with a nearby clean-up crew.

"Your Highness?" Risa spoke quietly into Jeremy's ear.

Jeremy immediately stopped what he was doing and looked into the little girl's light blue eyes. He sighed deeply and set her down. Kneeling in front of her as she sat upon the ground, he took her hand.

"Risa?" he spoke.

"Where is my brother?" she asked in a gentle voice, looking down at a pile of ash next to her. "Where is Kib?"

"Risa, I don't know how to tell you this," Jeremy began and took a deep breath. "But, Kib won't be coming back."

Risa tilted her head to the side, not understanding what she had been told. Then, she slowly placed her other hand on top of his.

"I understand where he is," she whispered.

Jeremy nodded his head and put his hand on her back gently. He then stood up and looked around for Jade. When he finally caught her in his sights, he reached down and took Risa's hand. The small five-year-old Pixadairie followed him as he approached Jade.

"All the children are now with their parental units," she informed him.

He nodded and raised his hand, carefully wiping dirt away from her cheek. She looked up at him and smiled, taking his hand in hers. Looking down at Risa, Jade sighed.

"I have got to talk to you," she addressed Jeremy as she looked at the young Pixadairie.

"Me too," he said quietly, looking around at the carnage left behind by the Cembalotes.

Jade knelt down to Risa and touched her damp cheek. "Risa, I would like you to go with Amber, okay?" she spoke softly.

Risa nodded her head and walked toward Amber. Taking her hand, Amber led her over to a few other Pixadairian children.

Jade then stood to her feet and looked up at Jeremy. "I may have a solution to our current problem," she informed him.

"And what's that?" he asked.

"Are you aware of what Amber can do?" she asked, looking over at the young girl.

Jeremy chuckled slightly and shook his head. "No," he answered. "You told me earlier in the bunker that she's your mother… and she wasn't dead after all," he spoke. "Uh… and that was hard enough to believe."

"It is all true, Jeremy," Jade professed. "Everything she has said… is the absolute truth."

"How can… how is it possible that Amber Drayke is your long-lost mother?" he asked, leaning down closer to her face.

"She just is," Jade whispered.

"I grew up with that girl, Jade," he argued. "I remember ten years ago when her parents brought her home from the hospital."

"I do not know how it is possible, Jeremy. But, it is," Jade said, visibly annoyed by his disbelief.

"Alright, let's say I believe this… this *story*, okay? I believe it. Now, what is your solution to our current problem?"

Jade scoffed and looked away from him.

"Jade, look… I'm sorry," he said and sighed. He turned her chin toward him gently. "I'm sorry. I've just had a really, *really* bad day."

Jade nodded her head and looked down at her belly. "I cannot fight in this condition," she spoke.

"I know," he said softly. "I agreed to let things go until after he's born."

"Well," she began and looked up at him. "I do not want to wait that long."

Jeremy paused and closed his eyes slightly, confused by what she had said. "What are you saying?" he asked her.

Jade took a deep breath and said, "Amber has the ability to reverse… or speed up the aging process in all living beings."

Jeremy was silent. He merely looked into Jade's green eyes, and waited for her to speak again.

"Jeremy?" she whispered, looking into his eyes.

"What are you conspiring to do?" he finally asked her.

"Our son will be easier to protect once he is born," she explained. "I cannot protect him in the condition that I am in. So, I want Amber to speed this process up."

Jeremy broke out into laughter. "You can't be serious!" he said, laughing. He threw his arms into the air and looked at her belly. "You hear that, Son?" he yelled, directed at his unborn child. "Your mother wants to speed up your aging process!"

"Jeremy, stop it!" Jade yelled and pushed him away from her. "Why are you acting this way?"

He immediately stopped laughing and placed one hand on his hip and the other on his lowered head. "Jade, a boy was just killed because of me!" he said, sobbing quietly. "And now, you want to risk our son's life by making him be born three months early."

"It will be okay," she whispered, holding his face in her hands. "Amber knows what she is doing," she said. "But, I will not go through with this if you are not behind me all the way."

Just then, Amber walked over and stood in front of Jeremy. "It'll be fine, Jeremy," she told him. "I would never hurt my only grandson."

Jeremy chuckled slightly as she spoke. He wiped the tear from his cheek and knelt down to look into her yellowish-brown eyes. "You're ten years old… and already a grandmother," he said and laughed.

"What's wrong with him?" Amber asked Jade, looking up at her.

"He has been through a lot," she answered. "We all have."

"Jeremy," Amber said and placed her hand on the side of his face. He sniffled and wiped a tear from his eye. "Your son will be alright… along with Jade," she whispered. "But, I will not do this unless you're okay with it."

"How can I be okay with this?" he asked her. "You're going to take three months of life away from him!"

"He won't even know it," Amber claimed.

"And he'll be okay?" he asked, looking at Jade's belly once again.

"Yes," Amber replied. "He'll be perfectly fine."

Jeremy sighed deeply and looked up into Jade's face. "Okay," he said, nodding his head. "Let our son be born."

"Are we almost there yet?" Eddie asked, leaning over the pilot's chair.

"Just about," Reet answered and sighed. "We could have had Sheila teleport us, you know?" he said, chuckling.

Sheila laughed as well and said, "where would be the fun in that?"

"You wouldn't find that fun?" Eddie asked her, jokingly.

Sheila laughed and shook her head. "Sometimes it's nice to be the passenger for once, you know?"

"Yeah, we're just messing with you," he said and sat back down beside her.

"I know," she replied and smiled.

"How did you receive powers?" Mariette asked suddenly, looking back at the two teenagers.

"Well, Sheila gave us our powers," Eddie answered, looking over at her. "As for her… who knows?"

"Sheila?" Mariette asked.

"Uh… well, it's kind of a long story," Sheila answered.

"I think we have some time, Sheila," Eddie added. "I've always wanted to know, too."

Sheila chuckled nervously and raised her hand to her forehead. "I'm sorry, Eddie... but, I really don't want to get into that right now... if that's okay," she whispered, looking over at him.

"Umm... okay," Eddie said, uncertain about her sudden hesitation. "You know we're all friends here, right?"

"Of course," she answered. "It's just... it's complicated."

"Okay. Maybe later, then?" he asked quietly.

"Sure," she said and smiled.

Just then, Eddie reached down and took her hand in his. He took a deep breath and looked into her dark eyes. "Sheila, can I talk to you for a second? You know, back there?" he asked, pointing toward the back of the airship with his head.

"Okay, sure," she said and stood up. "I promise I will tell you everything later, Eddie," she told him as they walked toward the back.

"Oh, no," he said and chuckled. "This is something completely different," he said and stopped walking.

He looked at her directly in the face and smiled. Taking both of her hands in his, he took a deep breath.

"Eddie... what is it? You're worrying me here," she said and laughed nervously.

"It's nothing to be worried about," he said quietly. "It's- it's something I've been meaning to tell you for a long time."

"Oh, yeah?" she asked, intrigued by his statement.

"Yes... Sheila, I-" he started, before he was interrupted by a violent shift in the aircraft.

Sheila was knocked off her feet, while Matthew and Vexy ran toward the front of the aircraft to see what had happened. Eddie helped Sheila to her feet while the others shouted to one another over the deafening sound of the engines failing beneath them.

Sheila began to walk to the front, when Eddie pulled her back. She breathed heavily as she looked into his panicked face.

"I love you!" he shouted over the loud noises.

"What?!" she yelled, placing her hand around her ear to better hear him.

"I love you!" he repeated.

Again, she failed to hear him. As the plane shifted from left to right, the terrified passengers struggled to figure out the source to the problem.

"I've always loved you!" Eddie screamed, frustrated by his incredibly bad timing.

"I can't hear you!" Sheila shouted, shaking her head in frustration as well.

As the teenagers were being thrust about in the cabin of the aircraft, Sheila attempted to walk to the front once again. This time; however, Eddie grabbed onto her arm and pulled her close to him. He looked down into her face and bravely leaned in to kiss her.

Since she had not heard him confess his love for her, she hesitated to kiss him back; uncertain about his actions. Then, all of a sudden, she wrapped her arms around him and returned the gesture.

They were interrupted yet again, by the aircraft pitching downward at a rapid rate. Eddie and Sheila released their embrace and stared at one another. Matthew ran past them in a panic, holding his head in his hands.

"I can't do this again!" he shouted. "I can't do this without Jeremy!"

As the plane continued to crash, Mariette stood at the front of the plane and closed her eyes, raising her hands above her head. Instantly, the aircraft stopped in midair, thrusting the teenagers forward.

Their panicked breathing was the only sound heard as they leaned forward, looking out of the main window at the ground, just three inches from the nose of the aircraft.

"Wow," Matthew said, breathing hard. "That was certainly a close one."

"You're not kidding," Reet agreed.

Mariette sighed and said, "six left."

Eddie looked over at her and nodded his head. "Well, we certainly appreciate it. Thanks a million," he told her.

Mariette nodded her head as well. Vexy stood up from behind the co-pilot's chair and shook her head.

"What hit us?" she asked them.

"I don't necessarily think anything hit us," Reet answered.

"What makes you say that?" Matthew asked.

"Well, we're still intact, for one," he answered. "If something hit us, we would be in pieces."

"Good point," Matthew said and struggled to make his way to the side door.

He quickly pressed a few buttons on the key pad, and waited for the door to release. The others joined him, and waited for the ramp to lower.

"Is the plane going to stay like this?" Matthew asked of the vertical position that the plane had suddenly stopped in.

"Yes," Mariette answered.

"Good," he said and chuckled. "It would really suck if it decided to fall… now."

As the ramp finally lowered, the others waited patiently for Matthew to climb up first. As he made his way toward the beginning of the ramp, he suddenly stopped, causing Eddie to accidentally run into him.

"Hey!" Eddie said, looking up to see Matthew standing completely still, staring outside. "What is it?" Eddie asked him.

When Matthew failed to move, or answer him, Eddie pulled himself up onto the ramp and gazed outside as well. There, to his surprise, stood twelve Cembalote soldiers, aiming their weapons directly at him. Eddie swallowed hard and stared into their stone expressions.

"Out!" Timothy ordered, approaching the ramp of the aircraft.

"Eddie?" Sheila asked from inside the aircraft. "What is it?"

He did not answer her. Instead, he watched as Timothy continued to approach him. With a quick movement, Timothy pulled Eddie down from the ramp and aimed the ray gun into his face.

Matthew held his hands up to signal surrender, and jumped down from the ramp to the ground below. Sheila then stuck her head out of the door and gasped as she watched the soldiers push Matthew down onto his knees.

"Out!" Timothy ordered to her. "Out with the rest of you!"

Sheila closed her eyes and attempted to stop time. To her own dismay, once again, her power failed. She held her head in her hands and tried once again.

"Now!" Timothy shouted.

Sheila then sighed and jumped down from the ramp as well. A soldier approached her and lifted her to her feet. He then strapped a restraint on her wrists and pushed her to her knees as well.

Timothy continued to stand outside of the aircraft with his gun aimed at Eddie's head. After a few seconds, with no additional occupants exiting the aircraft, he motioned to one of his subordinates. The soldier walked toward him and pointed his own gun at Eddie's head.

Approaching the aircraft, Timothy carefully inspected the failed engine underneath the cabin. He then climbed onto the ramp and slowly looked into the cabin. Initially finding no one else onboard, he looked back at his subordinates. He shrugged his shoulders to them and proceeded to climb into the aircraft.

All of a sudden; however, Timothy fell to the ground and held his head with his hand. Breathing hard, he removed his hand and gasped when he saw blood transferred from his head onto his hand.

"Who is that?!" he shouted, searching the aircraft for his attacker.

There was no answer. Instead, he felt himself being lifted up and pushed against the side of the plane.

"You will order my friends to be released!" Reet spoke to him in a furious voice.

"Who are you?! Where are you?!" Timothy yelled, flailing his arms around to strike the culprit.

"Let's go!" Reet yelled and pulled Timothy by the arm. He grabbed the gun from Timothy's hand and aimed it to his temple.

As Timothy appeared on the ramp, his subordinates stood below and awaited their orders. Reet pushed Timothy to the ground and jumped down as well.

"Who's there?!" Mason called out to Reet from behind Matthew.

"It's the invisible spy!" Timothy yelled, as he was being led by the arm by Reet.

The Cembalote soldiers watched in bewilderment as Timothy approached them led by nothing but a ray gun aimed at his temple.

"Let my friends go!" Reet ordered to the soldiers.

The soldiers merely stood in place, continuing to watch their colonel walk toward them, being led by someone they could not see.

"Colonel La Croix!" Mason shouted at Timothy. "Where is he?!"

"To my right!" Timothy answered and immediately threw himself to the ground.

Mason aimed his gun in the direction at his colonel's right, and shot once. Instantly, the teenagers and Cembalotes heard a groan, followed by nothing.

"Reet!" Sheila called out and struggled with the soldier subduing her.

They continued to watch Timothy's ray gun levitate above the ground as Reet continued to hold it in his hands. Then, to their surprise, a stream of visible blood appeared and dripped to the ground.

"Get him!" Timothy ordered.

Immediately, three Cembalote soldiers ran toward Reet. One grabbed the gun from his hand, while the other two stared at the blood running down his side, forming a pool at his feet.

"Well? Arrest him!" Timothy shouted, standing to his feet.

Before they could arrest him; however, they heard something land on the ground hard. Then, looking down to the ground, they watched as a single stream of blood originated from an invisible body lying before them.

Sheila instantly began to sob, while Eddie and Matthew watched helplessly. Timothy stood at Reet's side and raised his hand to his mouth. He swallowed hard and turned to the others.

"B-bring them in," he said quietly about the teenagers. "We're to take them back."

His subordinates complied and led the teenagers to their airship, parked nearby. Timothy continued to stand above Reet's unseen body. Mason sighed deeply and knelt down to the invisible being.

"Colonel, I… I didn't mean to kill him," Mason spoke.

"No, I know," Timothy said. "I didn't want any of this to happen."

"Then why did you apply for colonel?" they heard Vexy ask him.

Instantly, they turned around to watch her emerge from the downed aircraft. Timothy lifted his ray gun and aimed it at her.

"What are you doing, Timothy?" she asked, laughing. "You're not going to shoot me."

"I have to take you in," he said and motioned to Mason to remove restraints from his belt hook.

"I'm sorry, Miss La Croix," Mason spoke, and approached her.

"Mason, you slap those restraints on me, that'll be the last thing you do," Vexy warned.

"Vexy, please... let this be simple," Timothy said. "I've got my own orders."

"Okay, if Shane put you up to this, you can just forget about it," she said, standing to face him. "Little bother, I will *own* you when this is over."

"Mason," Timothy repeated.

Mason then walked over and pulled Vexy's hands behind her back. She continued to stare her brother down while Mason attached the restraints.

"You're going to be very sorry for that," she told him. "Very sorry."

"I already am," Timothy replied and looked down at the ground. "Believe me."

"Yeah, well," Vexy started while Mason led her to their ship. "You'll be happy to know that there is a live Ladaquitte on board!"

"What?" Timothy asked and looked up.

"Yeah, it's true!" she yelled to him. "I knocked her out. She's unconscious, but alive!"

Timothy then turned to the vertical airship and scoffed. He then shook his head at Vexy's ridiculous claim. Turning back toward the latest unfortunate victim in the battle for the Black Onyx, he sighed and knelt down.

"I'm sorry," he whispered to the invisible body, completely outlined by blood. "I'm so terribly sorry."

He bowed his head to his unknown victim and stood to his feet. Taking a few steps toward his own ship, he stopped and turned to look at the vertical ship once again.

Pausing for a moment, he laughed and said, "yeah, right... a Ladaquitte." He shook his head and approached his airship.

Walking on board, he could hear Vexy protesting her arrest. He walked past the room that she was being held in, and toward the front of the airship. On the way there; however, he encountered the teenagers, restrained to chairs against the wall of the cabin. They were crying quietly, grieving the recent loss of a great friend. Timothy lowered his head and continued to walk past them, feeling their pain… and hating himself for what had happened.

TEN

Victory is Born

The airship traveled through two universes to finally arrive on Universe Four. The grieving occupants continued to think of nothing but their friend, who perished while trying to rescue them.

The side door opened, and three additional Cembalote soldiers climbed onto the airship and led each teenager from the ship onto a path leading to Shane's castle. The three teenagers did not bother to watch where they were being led. Their minds surrounded nothing but Reet, and what he tried to do for them.

"Colonel La Croix!" a soldier called out to Timothy from the entrance to the castle. "Welcome back!"

"It's good to be back," Timothy said quietly as he passed the soldier through the door.

Timothy continued down the hallway until he reached the last door on the left. He knocked on the closed door and awaited an answer from Shane.

"Come in!" Shane called out.

"Sir?" Timothy said as he closed the door behind him. "We honored your request."

"They're here?" he said and stood up from his chair. "Great."

"Sir, I've got to ask you," Timothy began and placed himself between Shane and the door. Shane stopped walking and looked into Timothy's gray eyes in confusion.

"Uh, have you forgotten who's running this show?" Shane asked him quietly, staring him down.

"No, Sir," Timothy replied and cleared his throat. "But, I've got you ask you... what are you planning to do with those kids?"

Shane scoffed and smirked at him. "What business is it of yours?"

"None, Sir... But, I don't want to see those kids get hurt," he bravely disclosed.

"Then you don't have to be present at the time," Shane said and pushed through him to get to the door. "I'm your superior, Colonel La Croix... and you *can* be replaced at any time," he said, walking through the door.

Eddie pulled at the restraints on his wrists as he sat on the ground of their concrete cell. Matthew sat in complete silence, while Sheila sobbed quietly.

"What do you think is going to happen to us?" Eddie finally spoke.

Matthew shook his head slowly. "I have no idea," he answered him.

Eddie stopped struggling with the restraints and looked at his friends. He took a deep breath and asked, "how were we able to see his blood?"

Sheila stopped sobbing and looked over at him. "How can you ask that?" she scoffed.

"No, he's right," Matthew said quietly. "By all accounts, we should not have been able to see anything of Reet... blood and all."

"Don't even say his name," Sheila whispered and placed her restrained hands to her face. "I can't bear it."

"What happened to Mariette?" Eddie asked, shaking his head. "Why didn't she help us... or Reet?" he asked and looked down.

"Maybe she's really a coward," Matthew replied. "Maybe she didn't want to waste another magic session on us."

"It doesn't matter... all these unanswered questions," Sheila said and leaned her head against the wall. "We're facing certain doom here... I think you should be more concerned with that."

"You know what, Sheila?" Matthew asked and laughed slightly. "It doesn't bother me in the least. I am tired of fighting. My only wish is that Shane makes it quick... that's all."

Eddie and Sheila looked over at him. "How can you just give up?" Sheila asked him, shaking her head.

"It's easy... I just did," he answered. "I don't have Jeremy now... he's got his own life. And, besides... didn't Queen Xoula say that we shouldn't lose one another?"

Eddie nodded his head.

"Right," Matthew continued. "How'd it go? Oh, yeah... if one becomes lost, then both are. That's it, right?" he asked them.

"Yeah, Matthew... That's it," Sheila whispered and looked down. "That's the prophecy, anyway."

"What prophecy?" he asked.

"The prophecy about the twins; The Frost and The Waterfall," she replied and looked up at him. "Huh... there's more to it than that, though."

"Really? Like what?" he asked, intrigued.

"It's just a legend that has been circulating through the universes for millions of years," she explained. "The Triads told me all about it. That's why I was pleased that you received the power of frost, and Jeremy received water."

"You really need to start explaining yourself," Eddie said, leaning in closer to her. "Other than being the long-lost Triadal sister... you've done a great job at keeping mystery around you."

"Now's not the time," she said and looked into his blue-green eyes. "I'm sorry. I want to tell you everything, believe me... But, now is really not the time."

"Okay," Eddie said and nodded his head. "Tell me everything later."

"Eddie?" Sheila abruptly asked, looking into his face. "What was that about back there on the plane?" she asked.

Eddie swallowed hard and opened his mouth to reply, but was stopped by the image of Shane standing in the doorway.

"Shane!" he yelled out, and struggled with his restraints once more.

"Yes, 'tis I," Shane said and laughed, pushing the door open.

Timothy followed him through the door and looked into the shocked teenagers' faces. Sheila looked up at him in disgust, while Eddie and Matthew continued to stare at Shane.

"Continue your story, Sheila," Shane addressed her. "We're all so very anxious to know how you became... you know... you."

"I wouldn't tell you anything," she said and shook her head at him.

"Eh, I don't really care, anyway," he said and smirked at her. "You probably won't live long enough to tell it."

After he spoke, the teenagers stopped breathing and looked up at him. Timothy stood straight up from leaning against the wall and looked over at Shane.

"You're going to kill us?" Matthew asked Shane quietly.

"Chances are..." Shane answered and nodded his head. "But, first... I need to go speak with someone. I just wanted to stop in and see how you were doing... You're comfortable? Can I get you anything?"

Matthew struggled to stand up. "Please don't hurt Vexy," he pleaded with Shane, who had turned to walk out the door.

Shane instantly laughed and turned around to him. "As far as you're concerned," he began. "She's already dead."

Jeremy gently rubbed Jade's forehead as she lay on the cot in the bunker. Her terrified expression caused Jeremy a great deal of uneasiness. But, he continued to comfort her as the thought of bringing his child into this world three months prematurely should be the right decision.

"I'm sorry that this has to happen in the bunker," Jeremy whispered to her. "But, I don't want to take the chance of anything happening to him... or you."

"It is okay," she replied. "I agree."

Amber then approached them with Risa at her side. "I really don't think she should be down here for this," she spoke, regarding the young Pixadairie.

"Uh-uh," Jeremy said and shook his head. "She's never leaving my side from this point on."

"Okay," Amber said and sighed. "I just don't think this is a healthy thing for her to witness."

"She will be okay," Jade said, looking over at Risa.

Risa smiled at her and walked over to Jeremy. She knelt down beside him and placed her head on his forearm. She did not understand what was about to happen, but that did not seem to bother her. She felt safe and secure around Jeremy, knowing that he would always protect her.

Amber took a deep breath and placed her hand on Jade's belly. She looked over at her and nodded her head.

"Are you ready?" she asked her. "This could go quickly… or it could take hours."

"You don't know for sure?" Jeremy asked, panicked.

"I've never sped up the age of an unborn baby before," she said and shrugged her shoulders.

"Oh, I think I'm changing my mind," Jeremy said and began to stand to his feet.

Jade quickly grabbed his arm and pulled him back down. "I want this to happen regardless of how long it takes, Jeremy," she told him. "I cannot protect him."

Jeremy lowered his head and sighed. "Okay, Jade... I'm with you," he said.

Shane opened the door to Vexy's cell and laughed at the sight of her, sitting at a table in the middle of the room with her head down.

"Don't you look pathetic," he said, closing the door after himself.

She looked up and scoffed. "How dare you treat me like I am one of *them*," she said, pointing to the door, referring to the teenagers.

"Oh, my fault… Weren't you the one that seemed to be warming up to Matthew?" he asked, sitting down across from her at the table.

"I was only doing that for *you*," she said, throwing her hands up. "And you had me arrested!" she yelled, showing him the restraints around her wrists.

"I only did so that those… *rejects* would think that you're still on their side," he said and stood up. He walked to her side of the table and pulled a switchblade from his pocket. Vexy backed away quickly when he flicked the blade open. "Don't worry," he said and laughed, sitting down beside her. "I'm not going to cut you."

With a quick motion, he cut the restraints from her wrists and placed the switchblade back into his pocket. He sighed deeply and took her hands in his.

"As long as we're still on the same page," he said and kissed her hand. "Restraints will never have to touch these hands again."

Vexy looked down and shook her head. "Then do not *ever* use me as your puppet again," she told him sternly.

Shane chuckled and rolled his eyes. "You realized that, did you?" he asked, referring to the parlor trick he pulled earlier.

"Yeah, I did," she said and smiled. "Although it was clever… I will not be a part of it again."

"You got my word," he said, pulling her close to him. "As long as you stay with me… and you're with me… through everything."

Vexy nodded her head and looked into his gray eyes. "I'm with you."

Timothy stood in the hall, peering into the teenagers' cell. He looked up and down the hall, watching for a sign of anyone approaching. Then, he bravely turned the key in the door and entered the cell.

"You!" Sheila yelled at him, struggling to stand up.

"Please," Timothy said and held his hand up to show he was unarmed. "I'm here to help."

"No, we don't want your help," she spoke. "You had Reet killed!"

"That was never my intention," he claimed. "Please, I feel awful about that."

"What about Mariette?" she asked him. "Did you have her killed too?"

Timothy stopped in his tracks. "Who is Mariette?" he asked her.

"She's our friend… she was on the plane as well," Sheila answered. "Is she dead too?"

Timothy scoffed and chuckled to himself. "Does she happen to be a Ladaquitte?" he asked them.

"Yeah! So what?" she asked.

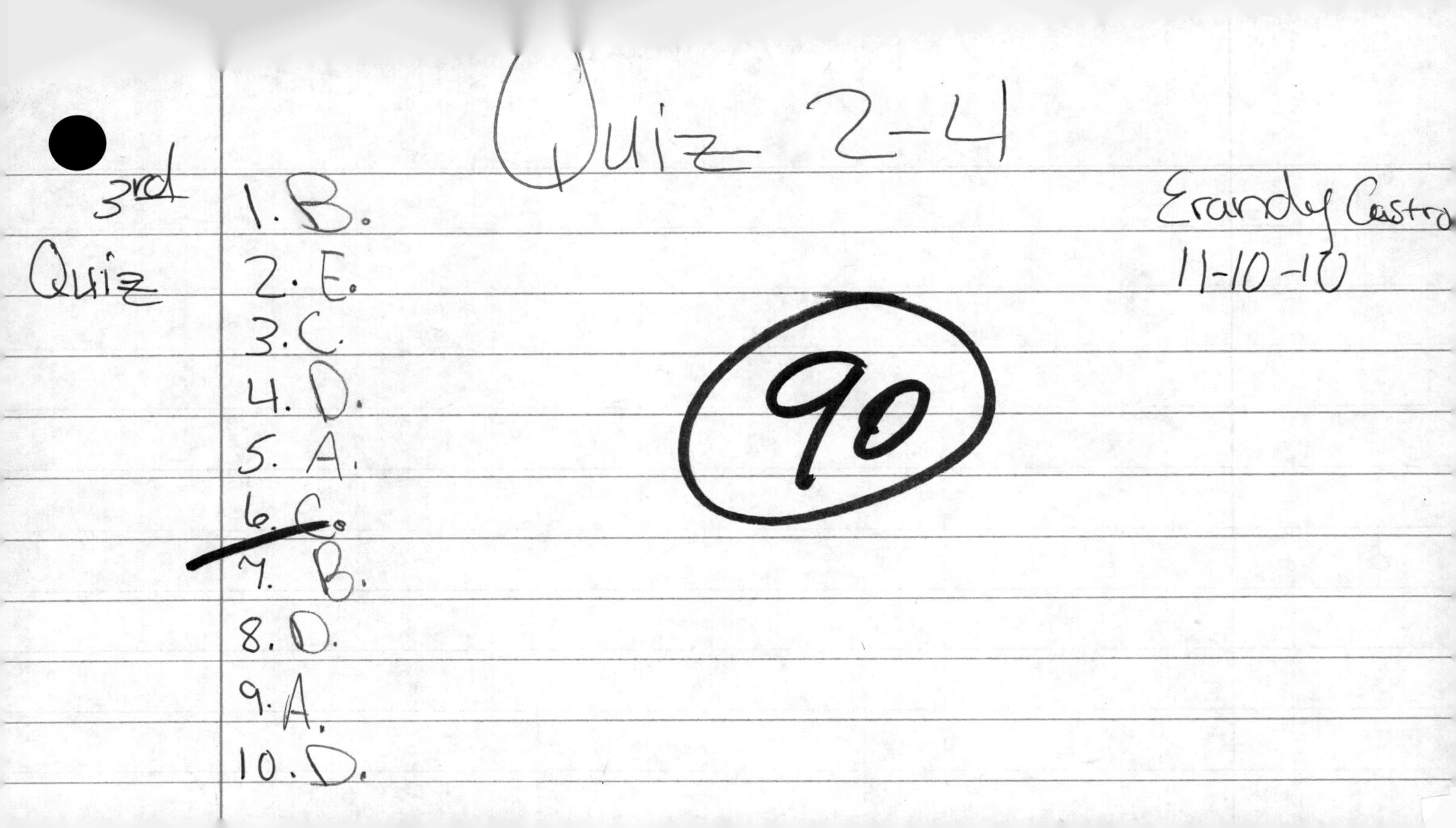
Quiz 2-4
3rd Quiz
Erandy Castro
11-10-10
1. B.
2. E.
3. C.
4. D.
5. A.
6. C.
7. B.
8. D.
9. A.
10. D.
90

"Then… she's perfectly safe… on the plane," he answered and approached her.

The teenagers watched him in silence as he cut Sheila's restraints. She rubbed her sore wrists and watched as he removed the restraints from Matthew and Eddie.

"Why are you helping us?" Eddie asked him, standing to his feet.

"I never wanted to be a part of this war," he explained. "My sister got me involved… But, the funny thing is… I didn't realize that once you join, you can never leave."

"You're Vexy's brother," Matthew said, standing up as well.

"Yes," he answered.

"Is she okay? Is Shane really going to kill her?" he asked impatiently.

Timothy looked at him and shook his head. "Shane will never kill her," he replied. "She's his wife."

The teenagers immediately looked at him in utter shock and dismay. Matthew laughed in disbelief, while Sheila and Eddie looked down at the floor of the cellar, struggling to understand the deception they had been the victims of.

"His wife?!" Matthew shouted, walking toward Timothy. "How can that be?"

"They were married four months ago," Timothy answered.

"But, Shane doesn't care about anyone or anything but himself," Eddie argued. "How could he possible be married… to someone else?"

"He was lucky enough to find someone who shares his evil plans," he told them. "You'd never believe it… since you have all seen a side of Vexy that I can only remember from memories… but, she is equal with him in hate and anger. She is the feminine version of Shane Aramay."

As this fact was revealed, the teenagers felt defeated. Not only was Shane the most evil being in existence… but, he found a counterpart almost as evil, and with the same motivation to destroy all that stood in their way.

"Well, come on, now," Timothy said and pointed to the door. "We've got to get you out of here somehow."

"Wait a minute!" Sheila said suddenly, and looked at her friends. "I can get us out of here now!"

"Well, I'm all for it," Matthew said and walked over to her. "I've had enough of this."

As Eddie approached them, the door to the cellar quickly opened, slamming against the wall behind it. The teenagers were startled, and looked up to see what had happened.

There, in the doorway, stood Shane and his new wife, Vexy. Timothy breathed heavily as he stared into the face of his sister.

"Timothy, what are you doing?" Vexy asked him, shaking her head.

"He was preparing us for your visit," Eddie interrupted, sparing Timothy from punishment for assisting them.

"Oh," Vexy said and smiled at her brother. "Fine job, then."

Timothy took a breath in relief and looked at Eddie. He nodded to him slightly, and turned, walking toward the door.

"I'll tell you what," Shane said and looked at Vexy and Timothy. "How about I take some time with my old friends, huh?"

Vexy and Timothy nodded their heads to him and walked to the door. Timothy stopped and turned to look at the teenagers. He knew that the teenagers did not stand a chance against Shane, especially since he possessed the Black Onyx… without their knowledge.

Jade anxiously watched Amber place her hands upon her belly. Amber closed her eyes and took a deep breath. Jeremy held onto Jade's hand tightly and waited for something to occur. Risa continued to shelter herself at Jeremy's side.

Within seconds, Amber's hands shook rapidly above Jade's abdomen. Jeremy's eyes widened with fear as his breathing increased. Jade sat straight up on the bed in pain and let out a deafening cry.

Jeremy stood to his feet and backed away, watching Amber's every movement. The little girl continued to keep her shaking hands situated above Jade's unborn baby. Then, to their astonishment, a bright yellowish-orange light emitted from under Amber's palm and pierced through Jade's abdomen.

Approaching the side of the cot, Jeremy looked down and gasped in delight as he witnessed the silhouette of his son inside Jade's womb.

"Oh, my God," he whispered, continuing to stare at his unborn son.

Jade continued to cry out in incredible pain as the baby began to grow rapidly inside of her. With the sudden excitement, Risa crawled underneath the cot and placed her hands on her ears, blocking out Jade's painful screaming.

Jade's abdomen began to expand outward as the baby continued to grow. She writhed and screamed in pain, keeping both of her hands situated on her expanding abdomen. Jeremy continued to watch the child aging at a fast pace. His jaw remained open as a single tear raced down his face.

With her hands shaking from the energy that she was pushing through them, Amber opened her eyes and smiled, holding her breath, as she too watched the baby increase in size and age.

"It's almost time," she spoke out.

"Oh, my," Jeremy whispered. "I can't wait to meet him."

"Shane… I beg you. Please spare our lives," Eddie pleaded to him. "We'll leave, and never return."

Shane laughed and looked at his former friends, huddled together against the wall of the cell. "I've come to tell you something," he said and reached into his shirt pocket. "I have something that allows me to feel no fear from any of you."

Eddie, Matthew, and Sheila stopped breathing and watched his every move. Then, to their astonishment, Shane pulled his hand from his pocket and held the Black Onyx up for them to see.

"See? I have the stone now," he told them. "So, you can't touch me."

"How did you get that?" Matthew asked, taking a step toward him.

"I had to do a little killin'," Shane answered. "But, it's mine now."

Matthew sobbed quietly and looked down. "What did you do to Jeremy?" he asked quietly.

"You wanna see Jeremy?" Shane asked him, putting the stone back in his pocket.

"What did you do to him?" Matthew repeated between sobs.

"Aw, quit your crying," Shane said and shook his head. "Jeremy's fine. I gave my word to leave them be if he handed the stone over. He did, so I kept my word."

Matthew looked up at him and wiped the tears from his eyes. "He's okay?"

"Yeah... matter of fact, he's about to be a daddy... officially," Shane informed them and raised his hands parallel to the ground.

Upon seeing Shane's sudden movement, Eddie and Matthew pushed Sheila behind them and began invoking their powers. Shane merely scoffed and rolled his eyes. A circular orb appeared in his outstretched hand and increased in size as he pulled his hands apart.

Then, an image appeared inside of the orb. Shane pushed his hands forward in one movement, thrusting the orb out from him. The orb disappeared and the images played out in front of them like a movie from a projector.

Eddie and Matthew stopped invoking their powers, and looked back at the wall of the cell. The images were that of Jeremy, Jade, and Amber. Matthew gasped and walked forward, staring at the present events taking place.

Shane smirked and tilted his head to the side, watching the images as well. "This is how I see things," he told them.

They watched as Amber continued to speed the baby's age up, hoping to allow him to be born quickly. Matthew smiled in delight as he saw the proud look upon his brother's face while he watched his son grow.

Sheila gently pushed through Eddie and stared at the miraculous event as well. Her expression changed to joy when she saw Jeremy's face. Eddie; however, watched his friends performing a strange power on Jade's abdomen.

"What is Amber doing to Jade?" he asked quietly.

"Oh, well... it appears that Amber is Jade's mother," Shane informed him.

All three teenagers looked back at him in bewilderment.

"Oh, I know, I know... I thought that same thing when I found out," he said and laughed.

Then, he waved his hand in front of himself, dissolving the images from the cell wall. He sighed deeply and looked at his old friends.

"What are your plans now, Shane?" Eddie asked him.

"Isn't it obvious?" Sheila spoke out, standing in front of Eddie and staring at Shane. "He's going to go after Jeremy and Jade's baby."

"Oh, I am not," Shane said and shook his head. "I have what I want. So, I have no further use for them… or you."

"You're going to let us go?" Matthew asked him.

"Probably not," Shane said and leaned against the wall. "Not sure yet."

"What's the hold up, Shane?" Sheila asked him, taking a step toward him. "We know that you have no intentions of letting us go… We also know that you could have accessed the Black Onyx with *no* problem before. You didn't need to torture us over it."

"What the hell are you talking about?" he asked her.

"What is it you're always reminding us about? Huh? You have infinite powers! You could have easily taken that stone from Jeremy and Jade at any time!" she shouted.

"Yeah, you're right," he said and laughed. "But, I like a good challenge."

"There was never any challenge for you," she said. "You just like to torture and kill. That's a fun time for you, isn't it? You can never make anything easy. You don't even need an army! But, you like holding people against their will, don't you?"

Eddie slowly put his hand on Sheila's shoulder to inform her to calm down. She merely turned around and shook her head at him.

"Calm down," he whispered to her.

"No," she said sternly, looking directly in his eyes.

Then, to their surprise, Sheila's dark brown eyes began to alter to dark blue; glowing intently as her anger increased. Eddie backed away from her while he watched the brilliant blue aura surround her as it had on Artobealu earlier.

"Sheila," he whispered, watching the glowing around her brighten.

She smiled at him and nodded her head slowly. Matthew walked over to Eddie's side and stared at the glowing girl as well.

She turned away from them and looked at Shane in fury. He merely shook his head and chuckled, continuing to lean against the wall.

"What do you think you're going to do, huh?" he asked her. "You think just because you're glowing... that's supposed to scare me?"

"It should," she replied angrily.

"Well, don't waste your time, or energy," he said and stood straight up. "You can't touch me."

"That's where you're wrong," she spoke, her voice suddenly altering from sweet-natured to furious. "You do not know the extent of *my* powers," she said, smirking at him.

"Is that right?" he asked, raising his right hand parallel to his shoulder.

Shane's sudden movement did not deter Sheila's intentions. She continued to stare at him, taking a step forward. With his palm open, turned toward her, he focused on creating a weapon.

Eddie and Matthew stood behind Sheila and watched anxiously as a long sword emerged from the center of Shane's palm. Quickly, he turned his hand toward the side of his face, grasping the sharp weapon before it fell to the ground.

"You know," Shane started, holding the sword in his hand, ready to use it against her. "I never liked you. I never even liked you *before* we all found out who you really are. You know why? Ever since you moved into our neighborhood... my mother would never leave the house without someone there to accompany her."

Eddie and Matthew stood in silence, surprised by Shane's statement.

"Yeah, it's true," he continued. "For some reason... she was terrified. It took me two months to figure out the real reason."

"Which was?" Sheila asked, taking an additional step toward him.

"It was you," he revealed and looked down at the floor of the cell. "My father left us because of you."

"Not because of me," Sheila said, taking a step. "It was you... he knew what you were and what you would become."

"Don't you talk about my father!" he shouted, pulling his arm back with the sword gripped tightly in his hand.

He then launched the sword into the air, aiming it directly at her. With the sword spiraling toward her, Eddie took a deep breath in panic.

"No!" he shouted out, watching the sword flying through the air.

He pushed Sheila from the path of the twisting sword approaching quickly. Just then; however, all was silent. Matthew opened his eyes and gasped when he saw his best friend lying on the floor of the cell… with the deadly weapon through his chest.

"Eddie!" he instantly shouted, and ran to his side.

The bright blue aura surrounding Sheila slowly faded away as she blinked her eyes rapidly and looked down at what had happened. She shook her head quickly in an attempt to remember the past few minutes.

"Oh, no," she said quietly and fell to her knees at Eddie's side.

Eddie gasped for breath and looked up into her dark brown eyes. A tear streamed down her face as she took his hand in hers.

Shane breathed heavily and swallowed hard as he realized what he had just done. Without speaking a word, he lowered his head and watched while his former best friend was losing his life.

"Look what you did!" Matthew shouted in between sobs, looking up at Shane.

"It was meant for her," Shane told him quietly. "Not Eddie."

"It's too late for that now!" Matthew yelled. He took a deep breath and said, "you can fix it, Shane! Fix it!"

"I can't," he whispered. "I- I can't."

"You have infinite powers, you jerk! So, fix this!" Matthew demanded.

Shane merely shook his head slowly.

Eddie then let out a painful groan and gasped. He struggled to look up at Sheila, grabbing her hand tighter as the pain increased.

"I- I," he mumbled as he continued drowning in his own blood. He swallowed hard and looked into her face. "I love you," he whispered to her.

She sobbed and ran her hand through his light brown hair. "I've always loved you," she said quietly and smiled.

Eddie returned the smile and closed his eyes. He swallowed hard once again as his gasps for breath increased.

Matthew placed both hands over his eyes and sobbed. Shane sighed deeply and closed his eyes as Eddie's gasps suddenly slowed.

"Eddie!" Sheila yelled, shaking him while his eyes continued to gaze up at her. "Please!"

"Oh, Eddie," Matthew whispered, taking his hands from his eyes. "This was never supposed to happen to you."

Eddie blinked his eyes a few times as a stream of newly formed tears rushed down his cheek. He gasped loudly and looked up at Sheila and then to Matthew. He slowly nodded his head to both of his friends and closed his eyes.

"That's it, Jade! You can do it!" Amber shouted over Jade's screams of pain.

Jeremy stood at Jade's side and allowed her to squeeze the life out of his hand. He groaned slightly as she bore down and began to give life to their son. Within a few seconds, the distinct sound of a new life was heard. Jade let out a relieved sigh and looked over at Jeremy by her side.

"You did it," he said quietly, and kissed her hand.

Amber carried the crying baby over and handed him to Jeremy. Upon seeing his son for the first time, Jeremy's eyes filled with joyful tears. He cried in happiness as the baby's blue-green eyes fixed on him. Jeremy gently kissed the baby on his forehead and looked over at Jade.

He placed the baby in her arms and sat on the cot beside her. She smiled at her new son as he looked up at her. Looking over at Jeremy, a tear streamed down her face.

"We both did it," she told him.

The cooing infant looked up into his parent's faces and yawned. Jade carefully examined his tiny hand as he wrapped his fingers around her thumb.

"My goodness, what a grip!" she exclaimed and gasped at her son's unusual strength.

Jeremy laughed and attempted to free Jade's thumb from the baby's clutch. Risa then peered up from underneath the cot. Jeremy smiled at her and waved her over.

"Risa, come over here and look at the baby," he whispered to her.

She slowly walked over to him. He lifted her up to sit on the cot beside Jade as well. As she looked into the baby's face, she smiled. It had been the first time since the battle on Artobealu that the young Pixadairie had smiled.

"What's his name?" she asked in a quiet voice.

Jeremy and Jade looked at one another and nodded their heads.

"Victor," Jeremy answered. "His name is Victor."

Sheila sobbed loudly and placed her head against Eddie's forehead. Matthew stared into his friend's lifeless face and cried to himself. Shane sighed and looked at them.

"I'm going to give you the opportunity to get out of here," he informed them. "But if I ever see you again, either of you… you'll get the same treatment."

He then turned toward the door and reached for the handle. Matthew stood to his feet and invoked his power, aiming his frosted hand to Shane.

"Don't do it, Matthew," Shane whispered with his back to him. "Just don't."

Shane waited a few seconds, and then turned the door handle slowly, walking out of the room. The icy wind surrounding Matthew blew away as he stopped using his power. He then sobbed and placed his hands over his eyes once again.

Sheila continued to cry with her head against Eddie's. She reached down to grab his right hand and held onto it tightly. Matthew sighed and wiped the tears from his eyes. He then knelt down to her and swallowed hard.

"Sheila?" he spoke out, touching her on her shoulder.

"It's my fault, Matthew," she sobbed. "It's all my fault."

"No," he said, shaking his head. "Eddie loved you… he always had."

"I didn't know it," she said, looking up at him with her tear-filled eyes. She sobbed once again and said, "I've always loved him."

Matthew watched as she leaned down and kissed Eddie on his forehead.

"He would rather… die… than see anything bad happen to you," Matthew whispered to her. "So, I guess… in a way, it was his decision. This in turn, makes that not your fault."

"No," she sobbed. "It's still my fault."

"Sheila," Matthew started and took her hand. "We can't let his death be in vain. So, I suggest that we get out of here before Shane changes his mind."

Sheila looked up at him. "Where would you have us go?" she asked in between sobs.

Matthew paused and looked down at Eddie's lifeless body. "I want to take Eddie back… home," he answered quietly. "I want to give his parents closure."

"You know what that'll mean if we go back," she warned him.

"I'm willing to do that… for Eddie," he said and began to cry. He lowered his head and whispered, "he deserves that."

Sheila nodded her head and reached out for Matthew's hand. He slowly knelt down to her and grabbed her hand. The two teenagers then looked down at their fallen friend. They each took his hand as Sheila began to concentrate on transporting them back to Earth.

Matthew and Sheila opened their eyes and looked around their neighborhood of Bowling Green. The empty sound of silence was heard as they continued to kneel beside Eddie.

"Time has remained still," Sheila informed Matthew.

He stood to his feet and nodded his head. He then looked down at Eddie's body; lying on the road with a shiny metal sword impaled through his chest. He took a deep breath and turned his head.

"I'm ready for this," he told her.

Sheila nodded her head and looked back into Eddie's face. Slowly, she leaned down and kissed him on the lips.

"I'll always love you," she whispered to him. "Forever."

She then stood up and looked at Matthew. His face was chapped with tears, and his eyes remained watery from new tears forming.

"I've decided," she started, taking his hand in hers. "To become who I was always meant to be."

Matthew looked at her in confusion. "What?" he asked quietly.

"I will become Sapphire," she said.

"Are you sure?" he asked her.

She nodded her head and said, "yes. I am going to go back and get justice… for Eddie."

"I think Eddie would've liked that," he said and smiled at her.

"Are you going to be okay?" she asked him.

"Oh, yeah," he said and chuckled weakly. "I'll be fine."

"Matthew, be sure," she said and looked into his face. "You know they will not react to this lightly," she spoke and looked down at Eddie.

"I'm sure," he said and smiled. "Hey, I always wanted to go home, right?"

Sheila nodded her head and returned the smile. "Right."

"Just… please tell Jeremy that I love him, and I'll see him later, okay?" he asked her.

"Of course," she replied and kissed him on the cheek. "You're doing a very noble thing here… Eddie would be proud."

"So are you," he told her.

"I promise that we'll come back for you," she said and sighed deeply.

"You'd better," he said and laughed quietly.

Sheila flashed him a smile and looked down at Eddie. The brilliant blue aura surrounded her once again as she began her transformation. She looked up at Matthew and winked at him.

In that moment, the sounds of birds chirping were heard throughout the neighborhood once again. Matthew looked around to discover that Sheila had resumed time once again. He sighed deeply and knelt down to Eddie. He nodded his head at his old friend and placed his right hand upon the fallen hero's forearm. Then, as he looked back up to Sheila… she was gone.

Sheila Greise and the others will return in
"Unexpected Heroes: The Reign of Shane"

Watch for it...

Correspond with the author at:
myspace.com/Zeppelin201
and
myspace.com/unexpected_heroes

E-mail:
unexpected_heroes@yahoo.com

Website:
www.charlenehaines.com

Graphic Artist Melissa Saville contact:
www.melissasaville.com
melissa.saville@gmail.com

Photographer Brooke Long contact:
cbrookeslife@hotmail.com

Breinigsville, PA USA
01 October 2009
225075BV00001B/65/P